I was angry and didn't really mean to make that wish. OMG, what had I done?

Dinnertime in our kitchen was another battle in a continuing family war.

"Mr. Hartman tells me not only did you cut that day last week, but several of your teachers are concerned about you. You've always been an exemplary student, and now suddenly you're failing tests and not handing in homework. What is going on? I want to know."

"Maybe it's just a case of senioritis," Dad suggested. "You know how they slump off at the end of school once the college acceptances are in."

"Not our Ailene. She's always been conscientious about everything."

"Mother, I don't want to be *your* Ailene anymore. You act like you know everything. Well, you're wrong about a lot of things. It took me a long time to realize that. I was totally naïve." With that, she got up and left the table.

"What's wrong with her? What's happened to our wonderful girl?" Mother said, dissolving into tears.

Father went and put his arms around her.

I left them alone together and decided it was time Ailene and I had a real talk. Even if I couldn't take back my wish, I was determined to do something to make matters right.

Val Williams believes she will never be as pretty or popular as her older sister Ailene. When Ailene dumps her on an unfamiliar road after an argument, Val decides to ask directions of the only person she sees—an old woman engaged in a garage sale. Val purchases a music box that the old woman claims has magical qualities and will grant Val one wish. In a fit of pique, Val wishes that that her sister would stop being so perfect. When Ailene starts acting oddly, breaks up with her boyfriend, stops talking to her friends, starts dating a "bad" boy, and cuts classes, Val is troubled. She begins to fear she caused all this to happen by making her wish and suffers a guilty conscience. How she goes about setting matters right makes for some unusual complications and surprises.

In *Witch Wish* by Jacqueline Seewald, Val Williams is kicked out of the car by her sister, Ailene, on the way home from school. Although Val doesn't really mind walking since it's not that far, she isn't really sure where she is as Ailene had to take a detour and ended up on a lonely country road. So Val goes to the first house she sees where an old woman is having a garage sale. The old woman convinces Val to buy a music box that she says will grant Val one wish. When Val gets home, she argues with Ailene and accidentally wishes for Ailene to not be so perfect. So when Ailene starts acting strange, Val is terrified that her wish was the cause. A story of sibling rivalry in a dysfunctional family, this is a coming of age story that is as compelling as it is entertaining. ~ *Taylor Jones, The Review Team of Taylor Jones & Regan Murphy*

Witch Wish by Jacqueline Seewald is the story of an average fifteen-year-old girl with a beautiful older sister and a mother who clearly favors the older sibling. When Val argues with her older sister, Ailene, on the way home from school, Ailene pushes her out of the car and makes her walk home. Since Val is not exactly sure where she is, she stops to ask directions from an old woman having a yard sale from whom she buy a magical music box that will grant her one wish. The old woman cautions her that her wish cannot be taken back once she makes it, so she needs to choose her wish carefully. But when Val gets home, she is still angry at her sister and rashly wishes that Ailene wasn't so perfect. Val feels a funny sensation, and Ailene begins to act weird. She defies her mother, breaks up with her boyfriend, and even skips school. Val is afraid that her wish has cause her sister to act this way, but she doesn't know how to make it right. A coming-of-age story that is both poignant and compelling, *Witch Wish* is charming, intriguing, and very entertaining. A great read. ~ *Regan Murphy, The Review Team of Taylor Jones & Regan Murphy*

ACKNOWLEDGMENTS

I want to acknowledge the help provided to me by the editorial team at Black Opal Books. Their input has been invaluable.

Witch
Wish

Jacqueline Seewald

A Black Opal Books Publication

GENRE: YA/MAGIC/FANTASY

This is a work of fiction. Names, places, characters and incidents are either the product of the author's imagination or are used fictitiously, and any resemblance to any actual persons, living or dead, businesses, organizations, events or locales is entirely coincidental. All trademarks, service marks, registered trademarks, and registered service marks are the property of their respective owners and are used herein for identification purposes only. The publisher does not have any control over or assume any responsibility for author or third-party websites or their contents.

DEDICATION

This novel is dedicated to Monte who supports me in every possible way. It is also dedicated to four wonderful, unique young people: Abby, Ella, Jonah, and Leah.

Prologue

Central New Jersey, 1985:

My sister Ailene pulled the car to the side of the road, reached over, and opened the door on the passenger side. "Get out right now!" she hissed through gritted teeth.

"No way!"

"Yes way. You're an obnoxious brat. I don't have to put up with you, and I won't for another minute."

Maybe I had gone a tad overboard in the rude department today, but she'd deserved it. I had to stand and wait while she giggled and gossiped with her airhead friends by the lockers for what seemed like forever. I stood there being ignored and feeling like a leper. Then finally when she finally turned to me, all she said was: "Come on. Hurry up." Like she'd done me this great honor giving me a ride home.

Now she was all indignation. Well, I wasn't going to stand for it. "I'm not getting out of the car," I said.

Unfortunately, Ailene was taller and weighed more than I did. She shoved me out, hurled my backpack after me, and drove off, burning rubber. She didn't even look back. So there I stood at the side of a rural road with no idea exactly where I was.

Ailene had veered off the main highway when traffic stopped. There'd been an accident on the highway. No way of getting through any time soon. That pissed her off, too. She's not the most adaptable individual.

It was a warm afternoon. I didn't mind walking, but the road was totally unfamiliar. I'd have to travel back in the direction of the highway. From there, I could find my way. Maybe my sister had done me a favor. Anything was better than being around her. She found me annoying, but I felt the same way about her.

As I walked, I fantasized.

Cheerleader shot dead at football game—mystery as to who pulled trigger. As a student of journalism, I considered this possible headline. Were I to murder my sister, I wouldn't want to be caught.

Don't judge me in haste. If you had a sister like Ailene, you'd probably hate her too. I'd like to say Ailene was nasty, selfish, and spoiled, but it wouldn't be true. I have my share of faults. Lying isn't one of them. The truth? Ailene was polite, intelligent, beautiful, and even charming—when it suited her.

So why did I hate her? Maybe because she was everything I wished I could be but didn't think I ever would be.

Someone like Ailene, who was so much better than most people, you envied, idolized, or hated her. It wasn't easy living in the same home with perfection day after day.

A house came into my line of vision. It was an old Colonial with white clapboard shingles and black shutters that had paint peeling. There was an old woman sitting in a chair with all kinds of items set out on folding tables in cardboard boxes.

I guess she was having a garage sale. I figured I'd stop and ask for directions back to the highway. She was kind of creepy looking, dressed all in black. But she was the only person around.

So I walked over to her. She stood up, smiling through crooked yellowed teeth.

"I'm kind of lost," I said.

She nodded. "I can see that."

She had dark, penetrating eyes. She studied me in an eerie way that made my blood freeze.

"Can you direct me back to Route Five-Sixteen?"

"Certainly. But first why don't you look at these things I have for sale. They are unique."

"Sure," I said, figuring to humor the old gal.

I began looking around. She had a lot of weird stuff, old crap that I had no interest in. But I figured if I offered to buy something I maybe could get the directions quicker. So I glanced at the stuff on one of the tables. A polished wooden box caught my eye.

"I see you like my music box. Actually, I have a bit of a collection." She picked up the box and wound it up. "It plays *Fur Elise* by Beethoven."

I listened and liked what I heard. "How much does it cost?"

"Whatever you can afford."

I was surprised. I checked the pocket of my jeans. I had some allowance money with me but there wasn't much. "I've only got four dollars."

"Just the right amount," she assured me. "There is one thing about the box itself." She hesitated. "You see…how should I put this?…the box has a certain unusual quality. If I bestow ownership upon you, the music box will grant you a wish."

I blinked and stared at her open-mouthed. Clearly, the old lady was a few slices short of a loaf.

"Sure," I said, trying to appear agreeable and humor her. "Great."

"You don't believe me, do you?" She gave me a knowing smile. Then she laughed, except I swear it sounded more like a cackle. The wind lifted her long, steel-gray hair, giving her an otherworldly look. "It's all right. I don't mind. But I think I should warn you. Once you open the box and make a wish out loud, you won't be able to take it back. You get only one wish, you understand. So think carefully about it. Make certain you wish for something you truly want."

The way she looked at me was just plain scary. I handed her my crumpled dollar bills and took possession of the box. She gave me the directions back to the highway, and I walked home from there. I placed the music box into my backpack and forgot about it.

It was a long dusty walk home, and I silently cursed

my sister. I dumped my backpack in the front hall, eager to get a cold drink.

My sister walked into the foyer and looked down her nose at me. "Pick that up and put it where it belongs. You know Mom doesn't like you leaving your stuff around."

"I'm hot and tired," I said. I narrowed my eyes accusingly.

"Serves you right." She smiled for spite.

I picked up my backpack upside down. I guess it wasn't fully closed because the music box fell out, hitting the marble floor along with two of my textbooks. I picked up the box and looked it over, hoping it wasn't broken. I wound the mechanism but it didn't play the tune.

I opened it up. There was nothing inside but a red velvet lining.

"Get your junk out of here before Mom gets home. You are such a slob!"

I felt my cheeks start to burn. "You're so judgmental. I wish you weren't so perfect and made mistakes like the rest of us."

At that moment, I felt a strange vibration like a seismic tremor. My hands shook. I looked down and realized the sensation was coming from the box. All of a sudden it slammed shut. So weird! Was the old woman right? Was the box magical? If that was true, I'd met up with a real-live witch. I shook my head to clear it of such far-out notions. Impossible! Absurd! No such thing existed.

Without the exchange of another word with my sister, I carried my things upstairs to my bedroom, and then I tossed the music box into my closet, consigning it to the back area at the bottom. I never wanted to look at it again.

Chapter 1

On Saturday night, the doorbell rang slightly before seven in the evening. I answered it and found super stud Jimmy Saunders standing there. This was no surprise. Ailene had dated Jimmy for the past two years. Although Ailene hadn't dated him exclusively, he was her special boyfriend.

His friendly, open face greeted me with a questioning look. "Is Ailene ready?"

"Dreamer! She's upstairs, primping and fussing as usual."

He sighed and followed me to the recreation room where the evening news was blaring on the television set.

"Better dig into the trenches for a while," I told him.

He nodded his head in a resigned manner, the veteran of many such evenings.

"Want anything to eat or drink while you wait?"

Jim shook his head.

"Well, I'll tell Mom and Dad you're here." I sauntered off to the kitchen where the folks were sharing an after-dinner cup of coffee.

They both looked pleased to hear that Jimmy had arrived. My mother's eyes beamed like big blue headlights. Jimmy was just the kind of boy she wanted for Ailene: handsome, intelligent, well-mannered. My father and Jimmy discussed the political scene briefly while Mother went upstairs to personally let Ailene know that Jimmy was waiting for her.

When Ailene did walk into the room, all eyes turned to her in admiration. She looked like a princess in a fairy tale. Tall, slim, and regal, she could have been taken for a model or an actress.

"You look great," Jimmy said, expressing it for everyone.

Her natural blonde hair had a sheen to it, and her bright blue eyes sparkled like sapphires. But Ailene frowned at his compliment. "We better be going," she said in her soft, silky voice.

"Such a nice boy, don't you think?" Mother said, turning to Dad after they left. "Ailene has good taste in everything, including boys. We're very fortunate to have a daughter like that."

I knew it shouldn't have been, but I felt as though her comment were a knife twisting a wound in my heart. I turned and walked out of the room. Just because she complimented Ailene didn't mean that I should feel put down, I reasoned. But feelings aren't logical.

I decided to take a light jog around the neighborhood.

It was a beautiful May evening. The weather was mild. The air smelled like perfume. Still, I felt lonely. I thought about the way Jimmy looked at Ailene, the way everyone looked at Ailene, and I felt depressed. Why couldn't I be beautiful the way she was? I used to think it was only because she was more than two years older than me that she had the advantage. But since I got to high school, I realized it was something more. Here I was a sophomore, fifteen years old, and no boys were looking at me the way they looked at her. Ailene was already being asked out by lots of boys when she was my age. She could pick and choose. The evening had turned into night and lost its charm for me. I walked back to my house.

My father gave me an odd look when I returned to the family room. "We wondered where you were."

"Just taking a jog."

"You should have asked me along," he said.

"I wasn't lonely," I lied.

"As a favor," he responded, "because I need the exercise. I'm too good a cook." He smiled and patted his midsection. He wasn't really sensitive about his gut, which I found kind of endearing.

"It's better when you cook," I told him. "Mom always goes for that low-calorie health food gunk."

"I heard that," Mother said, coming into the room with a dish towel in her hand. "That gunk would do wonders for you if you stopped rebelling and ate nutritionally the way I do. I know you sneak unhealthy food when I'm not around. Your complexion would be so much better if you cut out greasy foods like potato chips and chocolate.

Your sister never has your problems because she eats sensibly."

I turned away from her. I hated it when she lectured me. "We can't all be beauty queens," I said.

My mother won several titles back in her youth. Even though she was older now, she kept herself in perfect shape. Ailene favored her, and I guess it bothered me. My complexion did show a zit every now and then—okay maybe two or three zits—while Ailene's face was radiant.

"Don't sneer. It's ugly. You could be much more attractive if you wanted to be. You should be wearing make-up, for instance. I don't know why you won't. Maybe you don't want your mother making suggestions to you, but Ailene could. And you should do something with your hair. That color, such a mousy brown! We could have it highlighted. It needs to be properly styled. Really, Val, when did you last wash or comb it? When did you even look in a mirror?"

"Gosh, Mommy dearest, why don't you tell me what you really think?" I rolled my eyes. "You're so superficial."

She zeroed in on me angrily. "Well, that's what boys are interested in, like it or not. And if you ever hope to have a boyfriend like Jimmy, you better start caring about how you look." It irritated her to no end that her younger daughter refused to pay attention to appearances.

I jutted my jaw. "Who says I need, or want, a boyfriend?"

That was like a matador whirling a red cape in front of a bull. She knew how to push my buttons but I knew how to get to her as well. The mother-storm gathered with amazing speed.

My father came between us then. "Jan, you can't tell her what to do. She's got to decide certain things for herself."

My mother's lovely face flushed blood red. "You're too easy with her." Then she sidestepped and got a bead on me, wagging an accusing finger. "You love to cause trouble, don't you?"

"Yep, that's me, local gunslinger."

I walked out of the room to avoid yet another pointless argument. I don't know why my mother and I have never been able to get along. She thought I did things to spite her. Well, okay, maybe I did, but it was mainly a defense mechanism. She was wrong about Dad though. For the most part, he stayed out of petty disputes. Self-protection, I guess. Poor guy was surrounded by women, outnumbered, and outmaneuvered. Both my parents obviously loved Ailene best, but at least Dad tried to be fair.

I went into my bedroom, my own private sanctuary. Things were the way I liked them there: controlled chaos, small-scale anarchy. My mother no longer came into my room. She hated it. She even gave the cleaning lady instructions that my room was not to be touched until I picked everything up from the floor. Naturally, I had no intention of doing that.

I did some studying and then watched TV on the little set in my room. Being alone was better than exchanging insults with my mother.

My friend Toni called around nine. We mainly talked

a bunch of junk, but it was nice hearing her voice. I could tell she wasn't in a great mood either. Toni never talked much about her family.

Yet I got the impression she had problems at home a lot worse than mine.

"So is Ailene out tonight?"

"Do birds fly? Do bears poop in the woods? Ailene hasn't missed a Saturday night since she had the flu in February. Of course, with all the boys who call, she can hardly help herself."

"But she's going out pretty steady with Jim Saunders, isn't she?"

"Yeah, him more than anyone else."

Toni sighed deeply. "Wouldn't it be great to be that pretty and that popular? I guess I'll never know."

"Don't sell yourself short."

I wasn't just being nice. Toni was a cute girl, petite and slim. The fact that her clothes were kind of shabby wasn't her fault. Her family was poor. Toni lived in the Beach area of town, which was skanky. But Toni was cool. She was intelligent, and, like me, she enjoyed reading.

"Did you start our assignment on *Lord of the Flies* yet?" she asked as if she knew what I had been thinking.

"Just the first chapter. Don't tell me you got further!"

She laughed. "You know me all right. I read half of it. It's not Stephen King, but it's really good stuff. Makes you ponder the nature of evil. Val, do you think some people are born bad?" She said it like she had someone in particular in mind.

"Don't know," I responded, "the Calvinists sure thought so, didn't they? Thinking of becoming a Puritan?"

"Not likely," Toni said.

"I'll read the book and let you know what I think. Maybe you could ask Mrs. Owens about it in class on Monday. She loves it when we ask her questions about the reading."

"No way! You can ask her for both of us." Toni was very shy in school.

We talked a while longer. Then I could hear her father shouting at her in the background, and Toni quickly got off the phone. I picked up *Lord of the Flies* and began reading. A knock at my door interrupted me. I called out to enter and in walked my father, glancing around disapprovingly.

"When are you going to straighten up in here? People are starting to confuse this room for the city dump. Sloppy people lack focus. Slovenliness is a poor habit."

I let out a deep sigh. "Now you sound just like Mom."

He frowned at me, little wrinkles forming at the corners of his hazel eyes, the color I inherited instead of Mom's sky blue. "Your mother does have a point, you know. I wish you'd try to meet her half-way instead of being so rebellious."

"Me? She's the one! She thinks she knows everything. It's so annoying."

"Since she's your mother, she deserves your respect. You live in our house, you need to follow our rules."

"Yeah, whatever."

Dad's features set into hard lines, so unlike him. I got the vibe. So that was the way it was going to be. Mom had told Dad to be strict with me. She'd made him feel guilty, and he was susceptible to that. But when I didn't answer him, he relented. Occasionally, I recognized the advantage of silence.

"I didn't come up here to argue with you. Your mother wants to catch the late show at the movies. We're going to leave right away. I want to know if you would like to come with us."

"No, I'm reading this book for English. I'm really absorbed in it. Thanks, but you better go without me."

He studied me carefully. "All right, if that's what you want."

I always felt like a third wheel when I was with my parents. When Ailene was around, it was even worse. Dad added some reminders about house rules for when the parents were out and then left to get ready. A sense of relief whooshed through me. I was afraid for a few minutes he was going to insist I go.

About eleven, I heard someone come in downstairs. I knew it couldn't be the folks that early so it had to be Ailene and Jimmy. I quietly went down in my stocking feet and listened. Hearing Ailene and Jimmy in the rec room, I slipped into the living room.

Our house was a large Colonial set back on a cul-de-sac. Downstairs, beside a roomy kitchen and large dining room, a living room and rec room shared a common fireplace, one that was open on two sides. We hardly used the living room. Because of the open space underneath, someone who stood in one room by the mantle could hear everything that was said in the other room. In fact, if you just got down on your knees, you could even see everything that was going on in the other room. I guess by now it's pretty obvious I sometimes eavesdropped. I learned a lot of things this way I'd never have gotten to know otherwise.

Getting into the living room unobserved was easy because the staircase from the bedrooms led directly into the front foyer of our house, and from there into the living room. I called it the plastic room because my mother had all the chairs and the sectional sofa covered in clear plastic. The room was a showplace meant merely to impress guests. Mother had everything done in white. The carpeting was white shag. The chairs were white leather and the large sectional was alabaster velvet. If you stayed in there very long, it would make you snow-blind. The only person who'd be comfortable in there would be a yodeler from the Swiss Alps.

There were some large, impressive plants in the room, but they were all plastic too. Mother wouldn't take a chance on real plants. She only trusted the artificial kind. They were always perfectly groomed, never shedding leaves or withering.

The fancy cut glass tables and silver lamp bases helped make it a cold, impersonal place, but it inspired a sense of awe. In other words, no one used the living room much, except me when I was snooping.

I could see them clearly as I peeked through the fireplace. Ailene was making a busy job of putting her sweater and purse down on an end table. Jimmy took her by the hand and sat her down on the couch beside him.

"You seem far away tonight," he said to her.

She shrugged. "I don't know. I've had some things on my mind lately."

"What kind of things?" he asked, putting his arm around her shoulders.

"I don't really want to talk about it."

"Sometimes I find it hard to know you, Ailene."

"I'm not sure I know myself, so you're in good company."

He gave her one of those devastating smiles of his. "I certainly am." He leaned over and tried to kiss her, but Ailene resisted. "What's wrong?" he asked, the smile slowly replaced by a wary half-frown.

"Nothing, I'm just not in the mood."

He jumped up and began pacing the room. "Ailene, I don't understand. Is it that you don't like me getting serious about you? This all seemed to start when I gave you my varsity sweater and pin."

Her lower lip curled into a pout. "I know you think you're serious about me, but let's face it, we're only seniors in high school. We've both got years of school ahead of us, and we're going to be separated in the fall. I think it's a mistake for us to become involved, or even think we are."

He ran his hands over his short, sandy hair. "Say what you mean. Are you tired of me? Is that it?"

She stood up and faced him, her agitation nearly matching his. "No, Jimmy, I didn't say that. I like you more than any other boy I've ever dated, but that really isn't enough."

"Well, what is enough then?"

They were nearly nose-to-nose now.

"Look, try to understand. I was head cheerleader and you were captain of the football team. It was just natural we would date each other. It was kind of expected. We did what everyone wanted, followed the approved behavior pattern. But maybe, just maybe, we were wrong."

"Well, this isn't wrong." He tried to grab her and kiss her, but she pushed him away very hard. "What is this? We've been so close."

"Have we?" Ailene pulled back and crossed her arms protectively in front of her.

Jimmy straightened up to his full six feet. "If it's some other guy, I wish you'd just tell me straight out. I know a girl as pretty and popular as you can have every guy who looks at her at her feet."

"See, that's what I mean. You always think in surface terms like that!" She was pacing now and gesticulating wildly. Then she stopped and spun to face him. "I'm giving you back your sweater and your pin, Jim. It's over for us."

His hands became fists, and I could see the powerful muscles in his back rippling under his knit shirt. He looked like he wanted to punch somebody. "Just like that? Don't you understand how much I care about you? You think I'm just some dumb jock or something?"

Ailene shook her head, her golden mane of hair shimmering. "I never thought that. I never said it! I know how smart you are and how hard you had to work to be accepted to Princeton for the fall. I'm very proud of you. I do care for you, but it's not going to work out for us."

"Who is it? Some college guy? You looking for someone older, more mature?"

Ailene turned her back on him and folded her arms again. "I don't want to hear anymore of this, Jim. You're wrong. I've hardly dated anyone else since we started going together and you know it. Just accept my decision and leave me alone."

He pulled her around to face him. "I can't do that." His voice was choked by emotion.

Ailene was getting more agitated by the second. "Get out of here! Don't phone me anymore. I'm never going out with you again."

He stormed out the front door and slammed it after him. Then I heard the unmistakable sound of crying. Funny, I never thought of Ailene as crying about anything. She was always the cool ice princess, perfectly poised. Ailene breaking up with Jimmy, I didn't understand that at all. They were the All-American Teenage Couple, in large capital letters. What was going on in Ailene's pretty head?

I guess I wasn't paying attention because I smacked right into Mother's glass coffee table, the one with the very solid, carved silver sculpture supports.

My groan of pain as my shin hit the metal edge drew Ailene into the room like a homing device. Her tear-stained face reddened. I had a very bad feeling as she cornered me.

"You little sneak! You were listening all the time, weren't you?"

I backed away as she loomed over me, drawing closer and closer. Ailene looked positively homicidal. Her face wasn't so pretty right now, all red and blotchy like a blood sun. Her five-foot-eight form was imposing, like a precipice, over my five foot five frame.

"I—I just happened to be in h—here," I stammered.

Her index finger came up against my shoulder none too gently. She punctuated each declaration with another jab. "Don't hand me that garbage. You're slime! You're always lurking around. You probably enjoyed that, didn't you? You probably can't wait to tell Mom and Dad. Why can't you mind your own business? Get a life of your own." With that, she ran out of the room and up the stairs. Her bedroom door slammed behind her.

My hands were trembling after she left. I sat down hard on the plastic couch, then started to slide off and had to press down to keep from falling. Maybe I was no better than lizard leavings, always listening in on Ailene. She was right about me not having a social life, but I hated her for pointing it out to me. I decided that poor Jimmy didn't know how lucky he was to be rid of my ice queen sister. Still, I had to ask myself: if she really didn't care about Jimmy anymore, then what was Ailene crying about?

A terrible thought occurred to me. I had made a wish, however inadvertently. Sure, it was a mistake, but I had said I wished Ailene would stop being so perfect. Breaking up with Jimmy, her perfect boyfriend, could that be the result of my wish? But no, that couldn't happen. Right?

Chapter 2

On Monday morning, I took the bus to school instead of going with Ailene. I didn't think to ask, not after what had happened on Friday afternoon.

My parents bought Ailene a brand new Corvette for her seventeenth birthday. Ailene wanted red, but Mom insisted on white as being more appropriate for a young lady, as she put it. Dad agreed because he claimed that, statistically, police tended to stop red sports cars for speeding seventy percent more often than other colors. I think Dad makes up half the figures he quotes but I've never been able to prove it.

So Princess Ailene was driving around in an expensive sports car. She didn't offer me a ride, and I didn't ask her. There was a definite chill at our breakfast table but Mom and Dad didn't seem to notice. They were too busy getting ready for work.

Since Mom wasn't going nuts, it was obvious that

Ailene hadn't told our parents about her break-up with Jimmy. She knew how much they both liked him. I decided to keep my mouth closed. It was none of my concern. Besides, with the looks coming at me from Ailene, I probably wouldn't live to see sixteen if I breathed a word.

I did see Jimmy later as I walked to my biology class that morning. He looked preoccupied, and I don't think he noticed me. He was usually friendly and said hello. This morning, he just walked by, frowning at the world. I didn't see Ailene at all, which was just as well.

After English class, Toni and I went to lunch in the cafeteria. I generally tried to fix something for myself before I left in the morning, but Monday was tough. I was running late, so I'd grabbed a couple of dollars from the kitchen drawer for a cafeteria lunch and hoped for the best. "You buying?" I asked Toni.

She shook her head, holding up her brown paper bag.

"Got my peanut butter sandwich."

"I'll get you a milk."

"No, don't, I can't pay you for it. I don't have any change with me." Toni's large violet eyes cast downward under her dark lashes.

"What's a few cents between friends?"

I often bought her milk, even though I knew she couldn't pay me back. Maybe it was because her parents were poor or maybe they just didn't care, but the Walkers rarely saw to it that Toni had money on her. I knew Toni was ashamed of that fact. I think she could have qualified for the free lunch program, but for reasons I didn't understand, she'd never applied.

The lunch line was long as usual. The food smelled about as appetizing as week-old leftovers. So much for institutional cooking. The cafeteria reminded me of a scene in an old prison movie where the inmates rioted when they had to eat the cuisine. I ended up with a cheese sandwich. It looked better than the gray meatloaf and canned spinach that passed for the hot lunch special.

When I got back to the table, I quipped, "I wonder when the board of health will finally condemn our school kitchen, or is the penicillin mold growing on this cheese just part of a science experiment?" Toni just gave me a blank look. "Oh, well," I continued, "I suppose smart remarks have never been my strong suit."

"Sorry, I was just thinking about something else."

I handed her the milk, and we both started eating. As we did, I saw Jim go walking by. He glanced at me and continued then suddenly stopped and came over to our table.

"Has Ailene talked to you lately?" he asked, his dark blue eyes troubled.

I responded slowly and thoughtfully. "Not exactly, but I do know about what happened. If it makes any difference, I'm really sorry."

"Yeah, me too." He managed a wry smile, but it was fleeting. "Did she say anything to you about me? Anything about why she dumped me? I still don't understand it. I can hardly think about anything else. I can barely sit still in class."

Toni shot him a lightening-quick sympathetic look. I don't think he noticed.

"She isn't that open with me. Maybe she confided in one of her friends."

"I don't think so. They tell me she isn't even taking phone calls," he said, knifing his hand through his short, sandy hair. He gave a big sigh and walked away, shoving his hands dejectedly into his jeans pockets.

"Did Ailene really break up with him?" When I nodded, Toni stared at me in amazement. "I gave him my vote for Student Council President. He seems so smart and nice."

"He is. I don't understand it either. Still, Ailene must have her reasons."

We ate our lunch quietly, both of us locked into our own thoughts. When the bell sounded, we hurriedly cleaned up the debris and got ready to go our separate ways.

"Want to get together after school?" Toni asked.

"Can't," I told her. "There's a meeting of the newspaper staff. We have to get out one final edition before the end of school. Want to come along? You really ought to join the paper. You write so beautifully. It'll look good on your record for college applications."

"I won't be going to college," Toni said sadly. "My family can't afford it."

"Hey, you're smart. You can get a scholarship."

"No, and even if I could get one, my father would never let me go to college. He wants me to go to work as soon as possible and start to help out financially."

To say I was shocked would be an understatement. I stared in disbelief for a moment, and then realized what I was doing when Toni started fidgeting. I took a quick look around. Everyone was filing out of the cafeteria. Not a good time or place for personal discussions. "Let's talk about this again another time, okay?"

Toni nodded, obviously relieved, and hurried away. I felt bad that I'd made her uncomfortable. It was strange for me to think of Toni's parents not letting her go to college when my parents were just the reverse. My mother was always lecturing about how important it was to study and get good grades so that we could get into the best schools. My parents were going to pay a fortune so that Ailene could go to some snooty college in Boston. Personally, I would just as soon have gone to the state university. Mother, of course, considered that tacky. In New Jersey, where I lived, everyone who could afford it went out of state: It was practically a status symbol—unless of course, you get accepted to Princeton the way Jimmy did. But getting into an Ivy League college was definitely not easy. Even Jim said he was very lucky. I wasn't sure it was worth the trouble.

After school, I went to Mr. Schmidt, the newspaper advisor. He was a heavy-set, bald-headed teacher who suffered from terminal ring around the collar, but he knew a lot about journalism. Our staff had started out with about forty students but dwindled down to ten when the work assignments started coming out. We went over what we had to do for the final issue. Mr. Schmidt shook his head.

"We're short, as usual. Where's Williams?"

"Here," I called out.

"Val, get me an interview with Dave Greene. You know him?"

"No."

He squinted at me. "And you call yourself a newspaper reporter? Greene is graduating number one in the senior class. He's the valedictorian. Ask your sister, she'll tell you. He's just won a National Science Foundation Award, which entitles him to a full scholarship. Get all the particulars, and do it yesterday."

I've always hated that stupid phrase, but it seemed to make Mr. Schmidt feel like he was publishing *The New York Times*. Mr. Schmidt continued giving out assignments as I quickly left and headed upstairs to the science labs. I figured if this kid was such a brain, he might be hanging out there after school.

My logic actually paid off. I hit biology, then physics, and finally found Dave Greene in the chem lab, working on an experiment with Mr. Bascomb, the honors chemistry teacher. They both looked annoyed when I asked if I could borrow Dave for the interview. But I could be pretty persistent when I wanted something—as in pest. Actually, it didn't take much badgering at all to get Dave to condescend to give me a few minutes of his valuable time.

"We're in the middle of something important here," he told me as we walked out into the hallway, "but I can get away for a little while. What do you want to know?"

"First, I'm not trying to be annoying. The newspaper has a tight deadline. By the way, I'm Val Williams. You probably know my sister, Ailene. She's a senior, too."

He stared at me in disbelief. I knew exactly what he

was thinking and didn't like it one bit. People, especially teachers, had always compared me unfavorably to my sister, just the way Mom did. After a moment, he recovered and extended his hand, with a dawning smile. When I took his hand, he covered mine with the other one and held on a little too long.

"Sure, I know Ailene! She's been with me through four years of honors courses. In fact, I knew her back in elementary school. She's a really smart girl. If she wasn't so busy with cheerleading and social fluff stuff, she could be an outstanding scholar. Well, what is it that you want to know? I'll cooperate any way I can."

Funny how mentioning I was related to Ailene had completely softened his attitude. Whatever the cause, I took advantage of it and asked him a bunch of questions about the scholarship he'd won, writing busily as he talked. He seemed pretty nice, not at all conceited, as I'd expected. He wasn't half bad looking either, when he took his glasses off, which he did often. Cute for a nerd.

"I think I have enough for the article. Thanks. I'll let you get back to your experiment," I said finally.

He looked at me thoughtfully, brushing a lock of straight brown hair back from his long forehead. Then he smiled, and I noticed a dimple winking in his left cheek. "I've been unfair only giving you a few minutes of my time. Why don't we continue this interview another day? Maybe I could come over to your house tomorrow after school, when I'm free. How would that be?"

I stood up feeling awkward. "Okay," I said. I gave him directions for getting to my house, and he paid close attention. Was he interested in me? Why else would he want to continue with the interview? After all, it seemed like nothing more than a flimsy pretext for us getting together again. I didn't really know him so I didn't know how to react. Still, it made me smile thinking this senior, with his Einstein IQ, wanted to see me again.

I wanted to tell Toni about it, but she wasn't at home when I called. Her father answered, and he sounded so unpleasant that I decided to tell her about it the next day in school rather than call back.

But the next day, we didn't get together until gym class. While we were getting changed, I told her about Dave Greene.

"He sounds cool," she said.

"I hope so. I thought he'd be a creepy intellectual snob because he's so smart, but he didn't give me that impression. He wasn't snotty at all."

"Very promising," Toni said with a smile that lit up her heart-shaped face. She pulled off her long-sleeved blouse, and I noticed a massive bruise on her right forearm.

"God, how did you get that?"

Her eyes suddenly looked frightened, the long lashes quickly turning downward. "Accident, nothing at all. I'm clumsy, and I bump into things."

I eyed her doubtfully. It didn't seem to me that Toni was especially accident-prone, yet she always had bruises of one kind or another. "Your dad said you were out last night."

She frowned at me. "You called?"

"Yeah, I wanted to tell you about Dave Greene and see what you thought. Where were you?"

"Oh, out applying for a job."

I don't know why I was surprised, but I was. "How come?"

We were in our gym shorts by then and heading toward class.

"My dad says I have to start contributing. There was a sign in the supermarket that they're willing to train fifteen-year-olds. I'm almost sixteen. I got my papers, so I'm ready. They pay better than some places. My father thinks it's a good opportunity for me. I can work part-time now and full-time in the summer."

"But your school work will suffer."

Toni looked directly at me. "I can still pass. Lots of kids are working for spending money and extras. We need the money for groceries. My father's out of work a lot."

Toni seemed set on defending her position. Our gym teacher blew the whistle, and we had to line up. I suppose I had no right butting in anyway. It was time I realized that although we were friends, and had been since we got to know each other freshman year, Toni and I came from different worlds. Still, I couldn't help feeling that she was throwing away her chances.

I took the school bus home after school. For the first time since I could remember, I actually went up to my room, looked in the mirror, and neatly combed my hair. Then I went into Ailene's room and fooled around with the cosmetics on her dressing table. I put on a few dabs of her lilac fragrance, the one that always made her smell like spring. I touched my cheeks with blush and studied my reflection. Not bad! I would have tried the eyeliner, but I was afraid I'd mess up and end up looking like a raccoon. I was feeling pretty good about myself when I heard the doorbell ring and ran downstairs to answer it.

Sure enough, Dave Greene stood there, smiling eyes outlined in bold relief by dark-framed glasses.

I invited him into the rec room and offered him the available choices of cool drinks.

We decided on lemonade, and when I returned with it, he was looking around the room admiring the colonial decor and the orange carpet.

"You've got a beautiful home," he said. "I think this is about the nicest development in Wilson Township."

"Well, it certainly has big houses anyway."

He would have made Mother proud, if she heard him, but I never knew what to say to a comment like that. My mind was still busy in the background, contrasting my life with Toni's.

He drank the lemonade almost at a single gulp. "Good stuff," he said. "It's warm out there today."

"I was trying to think of what else I should ask you for the newspaper," I said.

He smiled, flashing the dimple again. His hand went to the pens shielded by his pocket protector. "If you like, I'll write out some things for you."

"That's okay. I can remember, although I forgot to ask you where you're going to school next year."

"Harvard," he said with satisfaction.

"That's terrific. I know how hard it is to get into."

"Not if you have high SATs and a straight-A average."

Just a tad too smug, I decided. "What kind of SATs, just for the record, so other students know what they need?"

"Perfect on the math section and close to it on the verbal. But I did study hard."

"I'm impressed," I admitted.

Even Ailene hadn't done that well. As for me, my PSATs weren't anywhere near the same league. "Do you spend a lot of time studying?"

"Almost all of it," he said earnestly. "I'm active in a few clubs like Future Scientists and the Academic Team, but outside of that, my time is completely devoted to schoolwork."

"No sports at all?"

"Taking gym is enough for me. I'm not very athletic." It was true; he didn't look anything like a jock, with a slight build, and no more than five-foot-seven at most.

"What about your social life?"

He flushed slightly, and I knew I had overreached the bounds of journalistic inquiry. "I won't put anything about it in the newspaper." I hastened to add, "I was just curious."

He shifted uncomfortably on the colonial sofa. "Truth is, I've never had much of a social life, but I intend to change that."

I smiled, setting my eyes shyly on the vivid orange carpet that picked up the pattern in the sofa's upholstery.

My pulse picked up a beat or two. "Well, that's good to hear. No man should be an island."

"John Donne."

"Who?" I said.

"The metaphysical poet who wrote that."

"Of course," I agreed. Was he going to ask me out on a date, I wondered?

Dave got to his feet and glanced out into the hall. I got the impression he was looking for someone. "Did you hear a noise?" he asked.

I told him that I hadn't. "My parents are at work. Dad's an accountant and works in Manhattan. He never gets home before six-thirty. And Mom is an executive assistant to a corporate vice-president. Sometimes, she works longer hours than he does."

"And Ailene? Where is she?" His eyes met mine. All at once, they seemed keen and sharp, like a steel blade.

Suddenly, I understood, and God, did it hurt! "Ailene probably won't be home until later. She's in a lot of activities at school. I think there were try-outs for new cheerleaders today. Ailene is involved in making the selections for next year." My voice dripped ice, but he seemed oblivious, too busy looking disappointed.

"So you think she won't be home until late?" For a bright guy, he was as easy to read as a picture book.

"If you came to see Ailene, you're out of luck. So why don't you just hit the road?" My voice was harsh, and his face was shocked.

He was saved the embarrassment of a reply because the doorbell rang at that moment. I hurried out of the rec room, glad to have an excuse to get away from the geek. I was angry and hurt and couldn't get out of there fast enough.

When I opened the front door, Jimmy was standing there, his head downcast and his hands shoved into the pockets of his jeans.

"Hi, Val, I came to see your sister. Is she at home?"

"No, she's not, but you can come in and wait if you like." *Take a number. Line forms at the left.*

He walked inside and then followed me to the rec room. "Do you know what time she'll be home?" he said in an agitated voice.

"No, I don't."

Jim caught sight of Dave then. "Hello, Greene, what are you doing here?"

"Val was interviewing me for the newspaper."

"But we're finished, so you can go now," I said pointedly. I turned my back on him and offered to get Jimmy a cold drink. He accepted gratefully.

When I came back from the kitchen, Dave Greene was still hanging around. I felt like screaming. I really wanted him to leave. I was furious with him! I handed a glass of lemonade to Jim who was talking politely with Dave.

"So how's the baseball team doing this year, Saunders?"

"We're holding our own."

"Aren't you supposed to be at practice or something?"

"I cut out today because I need to talk to Ailene. I couldn't concentrate on my pitching."

They looked odd standing together. Jimmy, so much

taller than Dave, almost looked like a father talking down to his son.

Jimmy turned to me. "How come you're not out for track this spring?"

I shrugged. "Pulled a tendon in the winter. I've still got trouble with it. I can't handle heavy mileage for a while, but I'm managing a couple of miles every few days."

Jim nodded his head gravely. "Good idea. You don't want to lose it no matter what."

"I'll be out for Girls' Cross Country in the fall."

The sound of someone coming into the house spun both of them toward the door. Dave and I followed Jim out to the hall. Ailene was just coming in, dropping her keys next to the Chinese vase on the glass hall table. Her cheeks flushed when she saw Jimmy.

"What are you doing here?"

Jimmy tried to take her arm, but she snatched it away.

"We have to talk. It's important." His voice was quiet but firm.

Ailene shook her head emphatically, her golden hair like a wheat field in the wind. "We've said it all. There's nothing left to talk about."

He faced her. "No, you've said it. I never got to say anything."

"Get out of here, Jimmy!" She turned and ran upstairs.

He took a few steps in that direction.

I think he might have followed her right to her room, but when he caught sight of me staring at him, he colored deeply.

He stepped closer, and his fierce eyes burned into mine. "Just tell her this isn't the end of it, okay?"

I nodded, and then he was gone.

Dave turned to me. "What was that about?"

"Hey, you're so smart. Figure it out for yourself." I still wanted him to leave.

"Let me guess: Ailene dropped him. Is she going with anyone else?"

I resented the question. "She isn't going with anybody that I know of right now."

Dave was suddenly all smiles. "Then she hasn't accepted a date for the senior prom yet?"

My eyes were hostile slits. "Just what difference does that make to you?"

"I've always liked Ailene, but she's always dated jocks like Saunders, so I never even asked her out. What was the point? I knew she'd turn me down. Maybe if I asked her now, she'd accept. Do you think she would?"

I was about to call him a vulture, but he looked so eager and innocent, I couldn't stay angry with him. I suddenly realized how badly I'd been behaving. He couldn't have known I thought he was interested in me, so he wouldn't have any idea he'd hurt my feelings.

"She might," I conceded.

But then his face fell. "I'm only kidding myself. She doesn't see me romantically. I know that."

"She might if she got to know you."

"How do I do that?"

I was thoughtful for a moment. "Well, you could come around here, I guess."

"I'd need a reason."

"To see me."

His eyebrows climbed up to ask me exactly why he would do that.

"Like, for instance, I need tutoring in geometry. My teacher says if I don't get some help quick, I might pull a D instead of a C for the year. That means summer school for me. I can get away with a C, but nothing lower. You could be my tutor for real. The National Honor Society members are supposed to do that stuff anyway, right?" When he agreed, I continued. "So it's perfect. You can be over here a lot. You can talk with Ailene, get acquainted, and when the time is right, ask her to the prom."

He seemed unconvinced. "I don't know. You really think it could work?"

"Put it this way: what have you got to lose?"

So it was decided that Dave would tutor me in geometry, especially when Ailene was home, and I agreed to let him know when that would be. Why was I being so nice to the nerd? I don't know. There was just something about him. Anyway, I really did need help with geometry. That wasn't a lie.

When Dave left, I went upstairs and knocked on Ailene's door. She didn't answer right away, but I decided to be pit bull persistent.

"Go away," she finally called out.

"Can't we talk?" I called back.

I heard her moving around inside the room. Then the door came open, and she stood there, beautiful blue eyes overflowing wells.

"What's wrong?"

She shook her head. "Seeing Jimmy here upset me."

"He's really crazy about you. He told me to tell you."

She threw herself on her bed. "He's just an immature kid that doesn't know anything."

"You're awfully hard on him."

"Listen, I don't want advice from my little brat sister. And the next time you interfere in my affairs, I'll break your scrawny neck."

That was it! I had gone out of my way to be nice to her, and here was Ailene, insulting me. She'd probably thought some awful things about me in the past, but she never talked that way to me before. Most of the time, she ignored me.

I stormed out of her room, determined never to be nice to her again. But later, when I finally calmed down, I realized that something was really wrong with Ailene, something that I didn't understand.

Chapter 3

B ecause my parents were late, I started dinner on my own. Ailene was still barricaded in her room, and it was probably just as well. There was hamburger meat in the refrigerator tray. I checked around and found the makings for Swedish meatballs and rice, a favorite dish of mine. Everything was almost done by the time my mother arrived.

"What's that I smell?" she asked on entering the kitchen.

"I fixed dinner tonight," I announced with a certain amount of pride. "Thought I could save you guys the trouble."

Her lips thinned in annoyance. "You used the chopped meat, didn't you? I wanted that for tomorrow. As a matter of fact, I bought scallops on the way home. Really, dear, I know you mean well, but sometimes you're such a nuisance."

I felt an ache in my throat. "It'll keep for tomorrow just fine," I said in a nearly inaudible voice. "Do what you like."

I never could please my mother, no matter what, so why did I try? I left the kitchen to her and went up to my room. I slipped into shorts and a T-shirt, the one I'd gotten at the last 5-K race I entered.

I needed to run. I hadn't jogged in two days. The sun was down now. It was the perfect time. I started easy and increased my pace. I ran all the way back to the high school, circled the track twice, and then ran back home, gradually easing my pace. I walked the last half mile to keep my muscles from tightening up. Nothing worse than leg cramps.

While I was running, I started to feel better about things. I felt the wind breezing through my hair and the air soaring through my lungs. I felt fully alive. I would break all the old records for girls' cross-country in the fall. I'd earn a scholarship for track. I wouldn't have to take any money from my parents for college. I'd be better than Ailene. Then they'd see that I was somebody, somebody special. I felt really on a high until I got home again.

"How's the running going?" my father asked with a smile. He was loosening his tie as I walked inside.

"My legs are starting to feel better."

"Have to get out there to the track one of these days myself," he said.

"Wish you would," I agreed.

"I used to be as skinny as you are once upon a time. Hard to believe now, isn't it?"

"Not really." Sure, my dad had developed a paunch, but he wasn't all that out of shape.

"Dinner's ready," my mother called out. I followed Dad into the kitchen. She was serving the scallops with corn on the cob and tossed salad. "We'll have your food tomorrow," she said in my direction. I didn't reply.

After serving, she looked at me closely. "Val, you're perspiring. You should have taken a shower before sitting down at the table."

"I thought it would add something to the ambiance."

"Must you always give a smart mouth answer for everything?" Her blue-green eyes darkened like a storm at sea.

"Better than a stupid answer, don't you think?"

My father smiled.

"Don't encourage her," she said with a warning scowl at Dad. "Val's never serious about anything." Mother called to Ailene to come down. "What's keeping her, I wonder?"

"Probably studying," Dad responded.

"Or on the phone with one of her friends. Honestly, they simply do not leave her alone! The phone never stops ringing." Then Mother turned to me again. "Val, you need to make more friends like your sister has. That trashy little girl, Terry whoever, is really not a proper friend for you. I don't understand why you bother with her."

My father tossed a hard look in her direction. "Jan, I can't believe you said that. Val's friend is a very sweet girl."

"But she has that certain look about her. I've seen it before on the faces of poor, neglected children. There are so many nicer girls, more appropriate friends for Val."

"Mother, I like *Toni*. As for Ailene, she has lots of acquaintances but very few real friends. There is a difference."

My mother's constant nagging and snobby attitude were just impossible at times. I was aware that, unlike Dad, she came from a very wealthy family. She was beautiful and pampered as a girl. Dad had won her with his warm heart and gentle disposition, but she never lost her sense of superiority. Her parents and sister were just the same. They always said that I looked like my Dad's side of the family. I know it was meant as a put-down, but that was fine with me. My father's relatives were much more loving and real. We just hardly ever got to see them because Mom always found some excuse to avoid visits.

Ailene joined us then and, much to my relief, Mother's attention turned completely to her.

"About time. Your dinner is getting cold."

Ailene seated herself. "Afraid I'm not very hungry, Mother," she said distantly.

"We're having sea scallops, your favorite."

"I believe Ailene prefers shrimp," I offered.

Mother pursed her lips as though she'd sampled something distasteful or maybe sucked on a lemon. "I didn't ask your opinion, Val." Then she noticed Ailene wasn't eating and immediately turned her attention back in that direction. "Is something wrong, dear?"

"No, I've just had some hard thinking to do recently."

"So have I. Do you realize that it's high time we thought about getting your dress for the prom?"

Ailene looked as if she'd just choked on a fishbone. "I'd rather not, at least not right away."

My mother tilted her head to one side in a gesture of appraisal. "Something is definitely wrong. Did you and Jimmy have an argument?"

"Sort of. Mother, Dad, I won't be seeing Jimmy anymore."

My parents exchanged a look. Both appeared alarmed. "But why?"

Ailene put her long, tapered fingers to her forehead. Her hands hid her face from view. "I can't talk about it, at least, not now. Let's just say, I might not be going to the prom, after all."

My mother looked as if nuclear war had just been announced. "Darling, don't even suggest such a thing! This is a once in a lifetime experience. If you miss it, you'll regret it forever. If Jimmy hasn't turned out to be the gentleman we thought he was, why, there are just tons of boys who would love to take you. Why don't you encourage one of the nicer ones? You can have your pick of dates. But don't let breaking up with Jim Saunders spoil this special time for you."

Ailene didn't reply. She merely nodded her head. My mother smiled victoriously, believing the matter settled to her satisfaction. After all, in the past, Ailene had always followed her advice. But the matter came to a head later that evening because of an unexpected phone call.

Chapter 4

The phone rang as my mother dished out a pint of fat-free vanilla yogurt for dessert. She was right in the middle of giving me a dirty look for mentioning I preferred ice cream.

The call turned out to be Ailene's friend, Vicky. Ailene shook her head at mother, silently refusing the call. Then she quickly left the kitchen. My mother seemed mystified but covered for her.

"Vicky, I'm sorry, Ailene is indisposed at the moment. Can I take a message and then have her call you back another time?"

My mother listened while Vicky talked. I could hear the oozing excitement of her voice, even from where I sat, but I couldn't make out what was being said.

I knew it pleased my mother by the big smile on her face. The sight of all those perfect white teeth was blinding.

"Yes, I'll be sure to tell her." As soon as she was off the phone, Mother called for Ailene in a loud, animated voice.

Ailene finally returned. "What is it, Mother?"

"I don't understand why you didn't take that call." Mother smoothed back a honey-colored curl from her face.

"I'm tired. I want to lie down. Vicky is only going to talk about silly, trivial things like she always does."

"Vicky is a good friend of yours. You know what she told me? Your name has been placed in nomination for prom queen. Isn't that lovely?" Mother's attractively painted face beamed with pride.

But Ailene, in contrast, looked fatigued and even dejected. "I told you, Mother. I'm not going to the senior prom, so it really doesn't matter."

My mother's face went from beaming to livid in record time. "I don't believe this! I'm going to have a talk with James Saunders and find out for myself what's been going on."

"Please, Mother, don't interfere. If you must know, it has nothing to do with Jimmy." Without another word, Ailene dashed out, ran up the stairs, and slammed her bedroom door.

"What do you make of this?" Mother asked my father.

He shook his head in bewilderment. "I don't know. It's just a phase, I guess."

That answer definitely didn't satisfy her. "Val goes through phases, but not our Ailene! She's sensible and mature. I could always count on her to listen to my good advice."

Mother looked really upset, but I was too busy being annoyed by her comment to feel sorry for her.

After a moment of silent yogurt spooning, I tried to relent. "If you want, I'll try and talk to Ailene about it," I offered.

Mother scowled at me. "I don't see how you, of all people, could be of any help."

I pushed away my glob of yogurt and stalked out of the room. I could hear my father's reproving voice as I left, but it didn't make up for the hurt.

⚬⚭⚬

I met Dave Greene in the school corridor on Wednesday between classes.

"What's new on the home front?" he asked eagerly. Of course, I knew he was referring to Ailene.

"When can you come over? I could use that help in geometry as soon as possible."

He appeared thoughtful. "Okay, I can make it this afternoon."

I didn't know why I wanted to see him. I knew he was only interested in finding out about Ailene, but for some weird reason, I wanted him around.

Toni and I discussed it over lunch. She really was the only person I could talk to about things. Despite her own personal problems, she always listened to mine. I wished she wasn't so guarded and secretive with me about her troubles, but I had gotten used to that. No one in my family ever really discussed anything outright either. It was considered shameful or weak to do that.

"Are you going over to the supermarket after school?"

Toni nodded. "So far, it's working out fine. The bus goes right past the store, and they're pretty nice to me there."

"Are you going to be a checker?"

"I hope so, except I've got lots to learn first. It's really a good job." She yawned, her lids closing languidly over her violet eyes.

"You're tired, aren't you?"

"I'll get used to it. I have to," she added, her lids fluttering open again.

"If there's anything I can do to help, like with homework, let me know."

She hesitated. "I could use your last two chapter summaries for English. I seem to be falling behind."

I opened my English folder, pulled the work out, and handed it to her. "For what they're worth," I said.

"Oh, you always do great summaries. Thanks," she said warmly.

I made Toni promise me that she'd let me know if I could help her in any other way. Then the bell rang, and we parted. I thought of Dave Greene coming over to my house after school and went through the rest of the day with a smile on my lips, though I knew it was lame.

Dave didn't arrive at the house until four, which was just as well. It gave me a chance to change my clothes and look in the mirror again. I decided to pilfer Ailene's closet, though she would have murdered me if she'd known. I found a beautiful pink silk blouse that I thought might fit, but when I put it on, it was way too big on top. Ailene had a blossoming figure while I appeared to be specializing in plane geometry. The pink blouse went back on its hanger and hung there, mocking me. I stuck my tongue out at it and went back to my own room. I put on a cotton-knit shirt that was at least clean—well, almost. Maybe Mother was right about the need to shop.

Dave Greene took off his glasses and wiped the sweat from his eyes as he walked into the foyer. "Kind of hot for May," he said.

That was my cue to be a good hostess and offer him a cold drink. We went into the kitchen, and I found some orange juice in the fridge. He accepted it gratefully.

"So what's been going on since we spoke last?"

"Want the good news or the bad news first?"

"Either," he said, fixing his eyes on mine.

"Well, you already know the good news, at least, I guess it is for you. Ailene refuses to date Jimmy anymore."

"Go on," he prodded me.

"The bad news is that she's decided she won't go to the prom at all, not with anybody."

At first, Dave looked totally discouraged. His mouth went slack, eyes got misty. Then he looked up, and the gloom cleared. "She could still change her mind. Ailene's always been social. My guess is whatever caused her to make this decision is going to pass over. A lot of guys will ask her, especially when they find out she and Jim

Saunders are through. She'll turn them all down. But shortly before the prom, she's going to be sorry and regret her decision. That's when I'll step into the scene. I'll pick just the right time, and she'll agree to go with me. I'll have the best date there! Everyone will envy me being with Ailene. What a way to leave Wilson High, in a blaze of glory." His eyes were glazed over contemplating his success, a smug smile in evidence on his face.

He really irked me big time. "A great victory for nerds everywhere, no doubt," I said caustically. "But aren't you getting a little bit ahead of yourself? How are you going to know just the right time to ask her, assuming that she'll really change her mind?"

"Oh, she will, I'm convinced of that. I've known Ailene since grade school. I understand her." He sounded disgustingly sure of himself.

"I don't think anyone understands what's going on with Ailene these days."

"I will," he assured me, "because it's all a matter of sensitivity and awareness. That's why having the right kind of intelligence is so important."

"Well, you may be smart, but no human being is omniscient."

"I didn't mean that kind of intelligence," he said with a hint of annoyance. "What I meant was that you're going to be my contact and keep me informed about everything that goes on with Ailene." He was looking off in another direction, fantasizing about his perfect date, no doubt.

I stared at him like a sideshow freak for a minute or so before I recovered. This was taking on the dimensions of some sort of diabolic plot. I was just realizing the extent of Dave's obsession with my sister. "Now why would I spy on Ailene for you?"

He spun around. Our eyes locked. His full attention was suddenly on me. "Because I'm going to be the best tutor you ever had! In fact, I'll help you with more than geometry. All you have to do is ask. Just as long as you do this one little favor for me. Do we have a deal?" He held out his hand to me.

I hesitated, but then I put my hand in his. "Yes," I replied.

Funny how the touch of his hand made mine tingle. An electric shockwave traveled up my arm. What a dummy! I pulled away from him immediately.

He noticed my sudden withdrawal and gave me a puzzled look. "You okay?" he asked.

For a moment, I couldn't find my voice. I just nodded.

"Fine, then let's begin our first tutoring session. Get your books."

I hardly noticed the time go by, but long shadows appeared in the family room where we worked, and eventually, I turned on the lamps. Ailene came home around five-thirty. I didn't bother to talk with her. She looked pale and out of sorts. Dave interrupted our work to say hello. They spoke together a few minutes, and then Ailene hurried upstairs. When Dave came back, his face was flushed. At first, he had trouble getting back to the problem we'd been working on.

"Hey, if this is too much for you, go home."

That upset him. "No, I'll stay until dinnertime, if that's all right with you."

There was no point in arguing, so we went back to geometry. My parents both got home around six, my mother first and then Dad. Dave was very friendly and polite to both of them. In fact, he made such a good impression that Mom invited him to stay for dinner. Of course, he accepted eagerly. Mother actually insisted that we eat in her elegant dining room, another room we rarely used. All through dinner, Dave tried to make small talk with Ailene, but she would barely speak. Ailene just pushed her food around on her plate.

Since Dave couldn't draw her out, he talked mostly with Mother instead. He told her all about his scientific studies and his goals for Harvard. Mother was terribly impressed. As far as she was concerned, having a Harvard pedigree would make Dave an aristocrat. She ate up every word like it was caviar. After he'd gone home, Mother turned to Dad.

"Awfully nice boy, don't you think, dear? I think he's going to be very successful in life. I also think he has a crush on our Ailene, don't you?" My father was reading *The Wall Street Journal* and didn't bother to respond, so she turned to me. "Val, will he be coming around to tutor you very often?"

"It looks that way."

She beamed with pleasure. "I must talk to Ailene about him."

My father put down his newspaper. I guess he'd heard Mother but was just ignoring the conversation until then.

He seemed to do that a lot. "Don't tell her anything. If she likes this boy, then she'll encourage him herself. She didn't seem very interested in him from what I could see." He picked his paper up again, shutting out Mother's inevitable argument. So instead, Mother left the room in a huff.

❧❧❧

Actually, Ailene didn't date anyone at all after breaking up with Jimmy. It was as if she completely lost interest in everything, including her vast male following. Ailene started coming straight home from school, closing her door, and moping around in her room. That was nothing like the Ailene I always knew and hated! Miss Perfect usually had a smile pasted on her stunning face, but not anymore. Lately, she could have passed for the tortured heroine in a gothic novel.

When Dave came by Friday afternoon, ostensibly to tutor me again, Ailene never even came out of her room at all. Dave spent most of our time together looking disappointed. Like Charlie Brown with his own personal rain cloud. It was kind of sad.

As he was getting ready to leave, he asked, "You will put in a good word for me with Ailene, won't you?" You could just see his self-assurance leaking away.

"Sure, I will. Come by again next week. Maybe she'll be more herself." My attempt to make him feel better seemed to work. He quickly agreed and then left.

On Saturday morning, Mom figured out a way to get Ailene moving. Ailene languished in her room, cocooned in her bed reading some book or other. Mother insisted I come in with her.

"Darling," she said to her first-born, "I need some help. Will you take your sister and do the marketing for us? I have a committee meeting for the League of Women Voters. You know how late those executive board things can run. Besides, it's a lovely day out there. It'll do you good to get some air."

Ailene nodded her head like a zombie. Her eyes looked dull and lifeless. Lethargically, she closed her book without bothering to mark her place. I noticed it was a volume of Emerson's essays. Definitely not like her to be reading something philosophical unless it was assigned homework. She wasn't acting like her old self at all. I had a really bad feeling. Was it my fault? Had I done this to her with my thoughtless wish?

No, it couldn't be! There was no such thing as magic. That was the stuff of fairy tales. I was feeling guilty for no reason.

Ailene drove out to the main road without uttering a word. She turned on the radio and pretended to listen to music, but I think it was an excuse not to talk. Once we were on the county highway, something happened to the car. Nothing drastic or dramatic, but the engine light went on, indicating a problem.

"Oh, no," Ailene moaned. "I guess I ought to take the car to Beck's. Dad always takes the cars there for service.

But it's out of the way, and they never do anything right off. They always insist on keeping the car."

"Well, maybe it's nothing much. Why don't we just drive in *there*?" I pointed to a service station that seemed fairly busy, but a sign said something about oil changes in a "jiffy." Ailene agreed and pulled into the station, driving the car around to the office.

"Stay here," she told me.

She didn't bother to shut the engine off. I saw her talking to an elderly man who wore worn coveralls. He disappeared for a moment and then reappeared with another guy who was obviously a mechanic, but he looked more like a professional body builder.

The mechanic came out and glanced inside at the red engine light. He shut off the engine and opened the hood. "Better get in the shade," he told us, "this might take a while." And of course, it did. But he looked capable.

When the young mechanic finished with the car, he wrote out a bill and gave it to Ailene. He had large dirty hands that touched Ailene's milky fingers for just a moment.

"What was wrong with it?" she asked, examining the bill in passing, then looking up at him with more animation than she had shown for days. His eyes were fixed intently on her face.

"Nothing much, just an oil leak. I did something temporary that'll hold it for a while." His resonant voice and self-assurance had us both riveted. "Bring it in for repairs soon. Matter of fact, you ought to have a complete tune-up done."

She nodded her head, not taking her eyes away from his. I could see why. He did have an interesting, charismatic face.

Suddenly, he turned his attention to me. "Say, kid, would you mind getting me a cola from that machine?" He handed me change, simply assuming I would.

Without saying a word, I took the money and left, feeling more than a little annoyed. As I came back with the can of soda in my hand, I saw the mechanic and Ailene still talking, his eyes glued on her face. He had a bold stare and a very macho look. His build reminded me of a young Arnold Schwarzenegger, broad, powerful, muscular. But the face was different. He had high cheekbones, dark curly hair, a neat mustache, and a small gold earring in his right ear. He looked like the kind of guy no one with any sense would mess with. He couldn't be much more than twenty, but he carried himself like a mature man.

I dawdled around, giving them a few more minutes to talk. I knew he'd only asked for the soda so he could be alone with Ailene. I wondered how, or when, she would go about brushing this guy off. No way was he her type. Ailene's taste, like Mother's, ran to clean-cut preppies, but she sure seemed fascinated. I had to admit, I could well understand the attraction.

When I finally came back into the office and handed him the soda, Ailene backed away a little, thanking him for his help.

"Anytime," he responded with a cocky grin. His dark eyes were bright and predatory as he watched us leave.

As the car turned toward the highway, taking him out of my field of vision, I released the breath I hadn't realized I was holding.

We finally made it to the supermarket and got the groceries. I ran into Toni, who was bagging, but we couldn't really talk because she was so busy working. On the way home, I brought up the subject of the mechanic to Ailene.

"The guy who fixed your car sure was interesting, don't you think?"

Ailene kept her eyes on the road. "The world is full of interesting people," she responded noncommittally.

I took the hint and turned on some music.

⸎⸎⸎

Late Sunday morning a guy called for Ailene. I answered the phone on the second ring and didn't recognize the voice, but it was unmistakably masculine, deep, and resonant. Of course, there was nothing unusual about guys calling Ailene, except that I could hear the warmth and animation in her voice when she spoke into the phone. That wasn't the Ailene we'd been living with lately!

"Yes, I certainly remember you," she said, her generous lips curving into a smile. Then she glanced over at me, eyes narrowing. "Just hold on. I want to take this call from my room," she said, throwing me a hard look as she headed for the stairs.

"I wasn't going to listen in."

"Then it would probably be the first time."

I held on until she picked the phone up in her room and then slammed the receiver down hard. She was on the phone at least a half an hour, because when I went to call Toni, she was still gabbing away.

When Ailene was finally off the phone, I called Toni and invited her to come over, but it turned out she had to work again. Her supermarket job was really taking a toll on her spare time. Still, I supposed it was something she had to do.

At noon, Dave Greene called. I was happy to hear his voice, but I didn't intend to let him know it.

"I thought maybe I could come over today," he said. "I finished up my work and thought you could use a little help."

"I could at that."

"By the way, is Ailene home?" I suppressed a groan.

"She's home and so are my parents. We're reading the Sunday papers." I felt like saying I'd save the comics for him since he was making a joke of himself mooning over Ailene, but for once I held my tongue.

Dave said he'd be coming over around two. We had casual lunch at one, just Swiss cheese and tomato sandwiches on toast. I was helping clear the dishes when Ailene started back to her room.

"Where are you going?" Mother asked. "You barely touched your lunch."

"I've got sort of a date for this afternoon, Mom. I want to change and get ready."

Mother looked pleased. "I'm glad you're finally getting over Jimmy. You need to get out. I've been concerned. You haven't been yourself lately. You're looking pale and thin. I was thinking a check-up with Dr. Larsen might be in order."

Ailene bit down on her lower lip. "I'm fine, really. I've just been doing some heavy thinking lately, is all."

"Well, introduce us to your date before you go. Is he anyone we know?"

"He's not from school. I doubt you would know him." With that, she was gone.

Dave arrived before Ailene's date. He was cheerful and friendly, as usual. Dad had put a baseball game on the TV in the rec room and invited Dave to join him while I collected my books.

"You like baseball?" Dad asked him.

Dave looked a little uneasy. "I'm not much into sports," he said. "My interests are more cerebral."

"I used to play sports a lot when I was your age," Dad said, "but now I've turned into more of a spectator than a player. That's what age does to people."

I looked into his hazel eyes flecked with dots of green and brown. "Only if you think that way, Dad. You have to come jogging with me soon. Remember, you promised."

He smiled, his eyes warm as toast. "I did, at that. But I think you ought to invite Dave. It's a nice sport to share."

I was surprised. It suddenly occurred to me that Dad thought I liked Dave and he was trying to help me.

"Running? Ugh!"

"It's good for your heart," I told Dave. "That is, if you have one." He frowned at me. "Just kidding," I said quickly, "no offense."

"Sure, no offense taken." But he still looked annoyed.

"Anyway, it would do you some good. Maybe after we study today, we could go. We wouldn't want you turning into a couch potato."

"I'm not wearing sneakers," he said.

"Another time then. It would firm up your body."

"I'm not flabby!" His tone was defensive.

"Oh, you're slender enough," I agreed, "but you need muscle tone as well."

"What about Ailene? Does she jog?"

"Not much, no."

"Maybe you ought to take up the sports she's involved in. It looks like she's doing something right."

I glared at him. "Rah-rah stuff isn't my idea of a sport. I prefer participating rather than cheering someone else on."

"You two want to battle it out with the dart board instead of your mouths? Dave, we've got billiards, ping pong, and darts set up in the basement. You can settle your differences down there."

"Fine with me," I said. Dave hesitated. "Afraid of competition?"

His eyebrows shot up. "I accept the challenge," he said formally, with an exaggerated bow.

"I'll be down to observe later," Dad said, turning to the financial section of the *Times*.

"No way," I told him. Then I dragged him off the couch to join us above his protests.

Dad's idea had been a good one. The three of us shot some pool and threw darts. It was a lot of fun. The inclusion of my father toned down my sharpness toward Dave, and he, in turn, loosened up a little, mostly because Dad put him at ease.

After an hour or so, Dad excused himself and left Dave and me alone to play ping-pong. It was a spirited match, which I eventually won, although he insisted that I was a cheat. When it was over, I led him back to the kitchen for cookies. Later, we went into the living room, and he helped me with geometry.

It was around four-thirty, and I had forgotten all about Ailene's date. Then the doorbell rang, and, when I went to answer it, the person I saw standing there made my mouth gape open in surprise—actually more like shock and amazement.

Chapter 5

"Hi, kid," he said with a broad smile, flashing pearly white teeth. "Go tell your sister I'm here." He followed me into the house, and I showed him to the living room.

"Who should I say is here?"

"Just tell her it's Ray."

Dave stood up, the geometry text falling to the floor. He gawked in surprise just as I had moments before. Dave with his thick glasses, knit shirt, and tweed slacks made a ludicrous contrast to Ray. Gone was the greasy mechanic's shirt and in its place was a black leather motorcycle jacket, open in the front, displaying a black rock concert T-shirt. His faded jeans were tight and torn slightly at one knee. He still had the gold earring on. I noticed for the first time there was a small scar on his forehead. It made him look fierce and formidable. His features looked chiseled out of solid granite, except for the eyes. They were very dark, bright, and alert.

Ailene was coming down the staircase, so I didn't need to get her after all. Her honey-gold hair was up in a ponytail, and she was dressed casually in short denim culottes and a red gingham shirt. She looked gorgeous, but then, when didn't she? Ray's eyes boldly caught hers.

"You're late," she said, but her smile made the criticism seem something else entirely.

"Someone had an emergency problem, so I did them a favor. That's the way it is with us car doctors. Better late than never, right? Ready to go?"

"Where?" she asked, her eyes still transfixed by his.

"Bowling alley?"

"I don't bowl." She folded her arms in a stubborn pose.

"So you'll learn. It'll be fun," he assured her.

She tossed him a dubious look but went to get a jacket. That was when Mom and Dad came into the room. I've never seen an expression on my mother's face quite like the one that bloomed there now. She looked dazed, like someone had punched her.

Her face turned a mottled unbecoming shade of purple. As for my father, red is definitely not the best color for his face. He looked like a slab of raw beef.

"These are my parents," Ailene said unnecessarily.

Ray extended his hand first to Mom, who stood there unmoving as a figure in a waxworks museum, then to Dad who shook hands numbly.

Dad was as speechless as Mom. The sight of their expressions was comical.

"Nice to meet you folks. I'm Ray Zanka." When they didn't respond, he turned to Ailene. "Ready to take a ride on my bike?"

"I'm not really dressed for it."

"Hey, I've got a second helmet. Don't worry, I'm careful."

"Maybe next time?" she suggested with a tentative look. "I'd like to take my car."

"Okay," he agreed, his smile easy. "I like my women liberated. You can drive me."

W all stood there staring after them, no one able to say anything for several minutes.

Finally, Dave spoke, his voice breaking the spell. "I guess I ought to be getting home," he said. As we moved toward the door, he said, "I'll come over during the week so we can work some more...Go figure." The last part was mumbled to himself. He shrugged, shaking his head as I showed him out.

When I came back to the living room, Mother had sunk into one of her plastic covered white chairs, something I never saw her do except when guests were present. The purple had faded, and now she was almost as pale as the chair. "My God, did you see *him*? I can't believe it!"

My dad turned on her angrily. "Jan, don't start. I don't want to hear it! I'll talk to her this evening when she gets back." He paused to stare at the door, as if seeing them leaving again. "Something is wrong. I have to agree Ailene's current choice of boys—or should I say men?—leaves something to be desired."

"How could you let her go out with that creature?

That…that…Neanderthal! Do you know how dangerous it could be?" Mother was furious. She never sputtered.

"You're blowing it out of proportion. Ailene will be fine. She's a sensible girl. I'll talk to her later."

"I know you. You'll just go along with it. You won't say anything. You won't do anything! I'm always the one who has to cope. I have to be the disciplinarian because you want to come off as the good parent."

"You're wrong, Jan." Dad's voice was deadly quiet, as if in warning.

"Am I? I always have to take the hard line, be the villain, because you refuse."

"I don't know what you're talking about. You're being ridiculous."

There was a wall of ice forming between them. Mother was standing now, stiff as a board. "I haven't forgotten how you handled that mouse and what I finally had to do about it."

He groaned at her. "Not that again! I'm not listening to this. I'm going out for a walk. Come on, Val, let's get some exercise."

I agreed to go and was grateful to do so. It was smart of him to get away. There was no reasoning with Mother right now. Their perfect daughter was being rebellious, and Mom and Dad were blaming each other. I grabbed a sweatshirt from the hall closet and followed Dad out. He agreed to my suggestion that we take a walk over to the high school track. We did very little talking along the way.

I agonized over Ailene's date with Ray Zanka. Was it

my fault? Had my wish caused it to happen? Was I to blame? *No, there's no such thing as magic*, I firmly told myself. I was feeling guilty when I shouldn't. I did my best to put it out of mind.

Instead, I remembered what my mother had said about the mouse. The memory made me shake my head. Mom had been alarmed when she found little black droppings in the basement during late autumn. I glanced at them and knew a mouse left them. We had white mice in the science lab, so seeing their droppings was not anything new to me. But Mom had been shocked.

"We do live by the woods," Dad had reminded her. "You wanted a house with a view. Everything has drawbacks. Field mice can crawl in during the winter."

But Mom wasn't about to just accept that. "I'll call the exterminators in," she said. "We've got to get rid of the vermin. They're vile. They can transmit diseases."

Dad wouldn't hear of calling in exterminators. He was opposed to the use of all pesticides and poisons. "They may get rid of the mice, but their methods are radical. Let me see if I can solve the problem first myself."

Mom gave in, and Dad went to the hardware store where he picked up the latest in mousetraps. Actually, he bought several of them. He called them humane mousetraps. He explained to me how they worked as he carefully cut small pieces of cheese and put one in each. The trap was left open, the cheese would draw in the tiny creature, and when it went inside, the trap would close. He could take the trap and release the mouse somewhere in the woods. Hopefully, it would never squeeze itself under the tiny area between garage floor and door again. Dad was very pleased with himself.

Several days passed and we checked the traps. The cheese was gone, but there was no sign of any mouse. Dad set the traps again. How could they get the cheese without getting caught in the traps?

Finally, Mom saw a small furry creature running between the basement and the kitchen. She let out the most ear-piercing scream I had ever heard. That was the end of it. The exterminators were called in against Dad's wishes.

They put out special poisoned food, which they explained, the mice would eat. It would make them so thirsty that they'd leave the house the way they had come in, running to the creek in the woods for water. And there they would die. It sounded good in theory. But as Dad pointed out, there was no actual assurance they'd leave the house after taking the bait.

One day not long after, Dad found a dead mouse in the basement. He called Mother to look at it. She was as appalled as he was, but not for the same reason. The whole incident created bad feelings between them, and I don't think it was ever fully resolved. Mom thought Dad was too soft, and Dad thought Mom was unfeeling.

This thing with Ailene was starting up hostilities between them all over again. I confess to taking a secret delight in my mother's frightened reaction to the mouse at that time. But my amusement had faded when my parents fought over it. I felt the same way now. I loved having my mother discover that Ailene, too, could be human and make mistakes. At least, in Mother's eyes, it was a mistake. Her precious angel was not so perfect now. That would teach her! Maybe she'd learn to appreciate me a little. But when I thought it over, I realized that was a fantasy as fantastic as Dave's obsession with Ailene. It was never going to happen. And I did hate to see my father looking so unhappy.

We walked to the track. Dad timed me for a mile run and then a quarter with me sprinting and kicking out at the end.

"That was very good," he said, handing me back my watch. "How is your leg feeling?"

"Better," I told him. "I'm going to run Cross Country in the fall again."

"We've got to get some meat on your bones over the summer. The running keeps you too thin."

"Well, at least I won't have to worry about dieting," I told him.

"Wish I could say that. Your mother's concerned about my weight." He was slipping back into the worry zone.

"Come on, Dad, once around with me, real slow," I coaxed. After a few minutes of playful argument, he finally agreed, and we did the quarter mile at a leisurely pace. I think we were both relaxed and feeling better by the time we walked home. Long shadows had fallen, and the twilight was purple satin sashed with pink, like a party dress. It felt good spending time with Dad.

But as soon as we got home, things started over again. Mom was in a foul mood. Dad's relaxed mood was gone as if it had never happened. For a long time, she wouldn't say anything and just threw tragic-heroine glances in our direction.

"Let's go out for dinner," Dad suggested.

"Absolutely not! I want to be home when she gets back. We've got to talk to her right away."

"I'll fix dinner," I said. I left them, as much to let them talk as to get away from Mom, and went out to the kitchen.

Ailene had picked out some very good chicken cutlets when we went to the market, so I got those out. There was a large jar of spaghetti sauce in the pantry. Nothing could taste too awful smothered in that stuff, so I put up water for spaghetti, and put some olive oil into a frying pan to heat. By the time I finished cutting up some lettuce and carrots for a salad, dinner was ready to eat. It gave me a feeling of accomplishment setting up dinner for my family.

Everything was fine until my glum-faced parents walked in and sat down.

"This chicken is tough. You over-cooked it," my mother complained, pushing her plate away. "And you know I don't like spaghetti. Carbs are fattening."

I started to say something but changed my mind. It probably wouldn't have mattered what I served, she'd still have complained.

Dad cleaned his plate with a piece of Italian bread. "Good meal," he said, "makes me feel better."

"Too many calories for you," Mother remarked.

They exchanged hostile looks, and he left the room. I tried to finish my meal with Mother glaring all the while.

After I'd choked down my food, I started to clean up.

"You can leave things as they are," Mom said.

"That's all right. I want to make things easier for you."

She looked so unhappy that I almost reached out to her.

"You'll probably break the dishes if I leave you in here alone."

That was more than I could stand. "Why are you taking it out on me because you're having a problem with Ailene? You're always criticizing me."

She turned away. "You're difficult. You have been since you were born, a colicky baby that wouldn't stop crying. You don't listen to me and never do what I ask. And now, Ailene is becoming just like you." Her face contorted with rage and disappointment, and although I knew she was a beautiful woman, right at this moment, she seemed ugly.

"Hey, I'm not the one out there with Wild Thing tonight, am I? I'm here offering to clean your kitchen, and you're spitting on me. Maybe I did crayon a few walls when I was a baby. Just how long am I going to have to pay for that? Maybe I do rebel against letting you pick out my clothes and against slathering myself in makeup every day. But I'm trying to meet you halfway, and you won't let me. Dictators always get overthrown eventually. Couldn't you be satisfied with just being our mom instead of trying to control every move we make?"

She turned her back to me, sobbing. I stomped out of the kitchen. As I reached the rec room, I heard the crash of a dish hitting the floor and more, even louder, sobbing. I wasn't about to go back. A sense of guilt hit me hard in the gut. Had I set this whole thing in motion with my stupid wish? I hoped not!

❧❧❧

My parents retired early that evening, around nine o'clock. It kind of surprised me because I thought they would wait downstairs for Ailene to return. But when she hadn't come back by eleven, even I was ready to call it a night.

A few minutes later, while I was going around turning off lights, I heard her car pull up in the driveway. I wondered if she would bring Ray into the house, but she didn't. They walked around together to the backyard. Dad had put the front and back lights on before going to bed. The lights were already off in the family room, and I left them off.

I could see and hear them perfectly through the sliding glass door. The thin orange curtain was translucent. I knew I was eavesdropping again, but I was couldn't stop myself.

Ray had a deep, resonant voice. It was a big contrast to Ailene's soft, silky voice. "Did you have a nice time?" he asked her.

"Very nice," she replied, with a smile. "I didn't think bowling could be so much fun. Thanks for the lessons. You're a good teacher."

"Anytime," he said, also smiling. "You're a terrific student. Is there going to be a next time for us?"

"Sure, if you like."

"Your parents don't like me."

She shrugged. "Does it matter?"

"Not to me, but I thought it might to you."

"It used to, but I'm changing."

He put his arms around her, drawing her closer. "Don't change too much. I like you the way you are."

He kissed her then. And I could see that the kiss was returned. When they came apart, they were both a little breathless.

"I want to spend more time with you," he said. "Only you have to tell me something. Why did you agree to go out with me? Seeing this house, and your parents, and their reaction to meeting me, I know I'm not the type of guy you're used to dating."

Ailene turned away from him. "Does that really matter?"

His heavily muscled arms gently turned her toward him again. "Yeah, I think it matters a lot, 'cause I could really get to care about you. But I'm not sure what you're feeling about me. In fact, I think maybe you're a little confused."

"I must resemble a window pane. Everybody thinks they can see right through me."

He touched her cheek with his fingers. "Not really."

"I guess I'm attracted to you because you're different, and it's important for me to be with someone who isn't like all the people I know. Maybe I'm tired of dating boys my parents approve of. Does it really matter?"

"Not sure I understand. What happens when the novelty wears off?"

"I don't know that it will."

They just stood there looking into each other's eyes, the way they had at the gas station. I could sense the intense feelings radiating between them.

It was like watching meat and potatoes simmer together on the stove.

"I'll let you go inside," he said. "I know you've got school tomorrow, and I have to be at work early too."

I saw them walk around toward the front of the house, arm in arm. Then I heard the motorcycle rev up and knew that Ray was on his way home.

I met Ailene as she walked into the hall.

"Mom and Dad want to talk to you," I told her.

"It can wait until morning," she said. "I'm tired now." Her face was attractively flushed, rose pink.

"It can't wait," Mother said, gliding down the staircase. She was cool and regal, dressed in an elegant apricot robe and matching slippers.

"It was pretty obvious to me, as well as Ray, that you disapproved of him. I never thought you and Dad were such snobs."

"You've never brought anyone like that home before, and I hope you never do again."

"There's nothing wrong with Ray. He's very nice."

"I want your father to hear this."

"I'll say it to him too."

My mother and sister confronted each other on the staircase, for a moment, fighting a wordless battle of blue eyes. Then Mother turned and rushed back upstairs to get my dad. Ailene followed her, and I followed Ailene.

"Why don't you just go to your room?" Ailene said sharply. "None of this concerns you."

I didn't reply, but I hung back a little. My father joined the two of them at the top of the stairs, looking like an arbitrator ready to negotiate a treaty between labor and management.

"Tell her how we feel!" Mother demanded.

Dad shot Mother a quelling look. "You can't go out with that boy—er, man—again. He's much too old for you." My father was clearly trying a different tactic. Being assertive had never been his style, and it didn't suit him now.

"Ray's only twenty. That doesn't make him too old for me. If he went to college, you'd certainly approve of him."

Father exchanged glances with Mother. "I suppose that's true," he agreed. "But he isn't the kind of young man we approve of for you."

"What kind is that?" she asked pointedly.

When my parents hesitated, I spoke up. "You always date preppies or jocks."

"Stay out of this," Ailene practically growled at me.

"That fellow is not our kind," Mother stated with emphasis. "He is trash."

"And you know that how? From meeting him for a moment? Really, Mother, you must be psychic."

"You can't date him, and that's final."

"Mother, you're being unreasonable."

"You'll do what we say! You won't see him again. You've disappointed me with your lack of good sense and judgment."

"Mother, you're such a hypocrite!"

"And just what do you mean by that?" Mother had her fists on her hips, full battle stance mode.

Ailene didn't reply. She just ran past them to her room and slammed the door shut. Nothing was really settled. Now Mother had a white-knuckle grip on the railing.

"Go to bed," she shouted at me.

As I walked down the hall to my room, I could hear my father talking quietly to her. I turned and watched them as I slowly opened my door.

"I don't think you handled it right, Jan. The more openly critical you are of this boy, the more she is going to want to date him. I don't want her doing things behind our backs."

"We can take back her car if she persists in this."

Dad shook his head, his forehead wrinkling worriedly. "It was a gift. It belongs to her now. We didn't make it conditional."

"At the time, there wasn't any reason to. But if it becomes necessary, we'll have to ground her."

Mother raised her eyebrows in my direction, and I ducked quickly into my room, closing the door behind me.

Suddenly Ailene was acting out, manifesting hostility and adolescent rebellion. Sure, lots of kids did behave that way, but not Princess Perfect. What was going on in her head? Something was really weird and wrong. Again, I couldn't help wondering if my wish was responsible. I feared that it might be, but common sense prevailed. No, something else had to have caused this dramatic sudden change in my sister. One way or another, I was determined to discover what was really responsible. I'd make like Nancy Drew and uncover the solution to this mystery.

I went to the window and looked up at the sky. I could see the face of a woman in the full moon, smiling with benign affection down on me as if to offer maternal approval. I pretended the face belonged to my real mother, the way I had when I was small. My mother in the moon radiated a kind, caring, loving persona, just the opposite of the drama queen who I lived with. It was a while before I finally laid down in bed or fell asleep.

Chapter 6

I took the bus to school on Monday morning, feeling really down. Sure, Mom's nagging wasn't exactly news, but my dad usually either ignored it or kidded her good naturedly. This morning, they were both pretty tense, as if each blamed the other for Ailene's strange behavior.

I dragged through the morning sleepy-eyed since I hadn't rested well. All night, I kept having crazy dreams—Ray becoming Dracula and biting my sister on the neck, my mother turning into a wicked witch, and my dad becoming a zombie. That was what I got for leaving the TV on all night and zoning into horror movies.

At lunch, Toni and I didn't do much talking at first. We just ate our sandwiches, and I shared a small bag of chips with her. Toni was tired, too. I didn't ask, but I knew she must have worked pretty hard over the weekend.

As we were finishing up, I noticed Jimmy Saunders looking over at me. I smiled at him, and that was enough encouragement for him to come over to our table.

"Hi, Val, can I talk to you for a minute?"

"Sure. What's up?"

Toni's eyebrows shot up. I saw the expression but knew she was wrong. If a good-looking guy wanted to talk to me, it had something to do with Ailene. So maybe I was cynical, but I knew the score.

"I guess you realize Ailene still won't see me, won't return any of my phone calls." I didn't answer, but he went on anyway, moving with unease in his chair. "I was thinking that there's got to be some way for me to reach her. I can't believe she s stopped caring about me, just like that." He snapped his fingers for emphasis. "This isn't easy for me. I guess what I'm saying is I'd appreciate any help you could give me. I need to get some insight into what she's thinking and feeling. You're the only one close enough to tell me that."

"I would help if I could," I said, "but she doesn't confide in me. You know that."

"Maybe you've overheard her say something?"

I blushed to the roots of my hair. He obviously thought I was a snoop. Well, wasn't I? "Look, Jimmy, the truth is, she doesn't even talk to Mom now. In fact, both my parents are upset with her."

Jimmy ran his right hand through the short shock of sandy hair. "She doesn't talk to any of her girlfriends anymore either. It's like she's cut herself off from everybody and everything that was important to her. You know she didn't even show up for the last Student Council meeting? That's not like Ailene. She's always been the most reliable, responsible person in our class. Something's wrong, and I've got to do something about it." He clenched his fist in a fit of determination.

"But what can you do?"

"You could help," he said, his tone earnest.

"How?"

"Keep me informed of what's going on with her."

This was the second guy who wanted me to spy on Ailene for him. I thought I saw a pattern forming here. Maybe I had a future with the CIA. "Okay," I agreed reluctantly. "But I don't see how it will help."

"One good thing, at least she hasn't been dating any of the other guys." He caught my surprised look before I could hide it.

I shifted in my chair. "Jim, there's something you ought to know. She has dated someone else." I saw his strong teeth clench together. "But just once," I added hastily. "And it was this mechanic who works at a gas station. It wasn't anyone from school."

"You know anything about this guy? Who he is? What kind of person?" Jimmy was oblivious to anything but our conversation. His intensity was drawing some stares.

"I don't know much. His name is Ray Zanka, and he looks older."

Jimmy was thoughtful. "Zanka, huh? I used to know a fella with that name a few years ago. Does he look like he might have wrestled?"

"And then some. Dark, curly hair, high cheekbones, kind of dangerous-looking."

"Yeah, that's him. We were both on the wrestling team. He was the best in his weight class. Coach said for sure he'd make it to the state finals. He won in the districts and the counties, our first real champ in years. Coach was sure he'd get a college scholarship. He was a smart wrestler, besides being physically powerful. He had all the right moves and sure instincts."

"What happened to him?" I asked. The guy Jim was describing didn't sound much like the character who'd taken Ailene out yesterday.

"Nobody really knows. Zanka just up and quit school one day."

"You're kidding!"

He gave me a look that said he wasn't but didn't understand it either. "It was strange. There he was on top of everything, a fierce dude with a killer instinct when he walked out on the mat. He'd earned everyone's respect. And then suddenly, he gave it all up. I never figured it out. No one did. Coach was beside himself, but Zanka wouldn't even discuss it with him, wouldn't say a word. He just walked away from a great future. It wasn't like he was stupid and flunking out. So now he pumps gas. Pitiful." Jim shook his head in disgust.

"He's a very good mechanic from what I can tell." I don't know why but I felt as though Ray deserved to be defended.

"I used to know Ray, too," Toni said in a quiet voice.

Jim and I both looked at her in surprise. It was the first time she'd spoken since he joined us at the lunch table.

"How did you know him?" Jim asked.

Toni glanced shyly at Jim. "Ray was friends with my brother Eddy. They were in the same classes. They hung out together sometimes. Ray was always real nice to me and my sister. But when Eddy left and joined the army, we kind of lost track of Ray. I guess he's got new friends now."

"Did he ride a motorcycle when you knew him?" I asked.

"Yeah, a Harley." Toni smiled as if the memory was a pleasant one.

"Face it," Jim said, suddenly angry, "the guy's a burn-out! I don't know what Ailene could be thinking of, taking up with someone like that. They don't have anything in common."

I remembered how they had kissed last night in the moonlight. They certainly did have something in common. But I wasn't about to say so in front of Jim. "Maybe I shouldn't have told you," I said.

He visibly forced himself to relax. "No, I wanted to know. I asked you. I can't believe she'll see him again. Just let me know what happens. It's very important to me."

After getting my promise that I would—against my better judgment—Jim walked off with his fists stuck in his pockets. I got busy cleaning up and checking the clock. The passing bell would ring in four minutes.

"He's wrong about Ray Zanka," Toni insisted quietly.

"Ray's really an okay guy. Maybe I'm prejudiced. He does come from Crawford's Beach, like me, but guys that are nice to younger kids when they don't have to be are usually good inside."

I trusted Toni's judgment in most things, but I wasn't convinced at all. Instead of answering, I started gathering up my books.

As we were getting ready to leave the cafeteria, Dave Greene walked by. I tapped his shoulder, and he turned around.

"Hi," I said, "remember me?"

"Sure, how could I forget?"

"Are we on for tutoring this week?"

"Tomorrow afternoon all right?"

"Are you in the next lunch period?"

He shook his head, and the straight lock of dark brown hair fell across his forehead. "I don't take a lunch. As I see it, lunch is a waste of valuable time. That goes for study hall too. So I just come in and buy something between periods. I have a lab next, and no one minds if I eat while I work."

"Sure, what's a little hydrochloric acid on rye anyway? Probably tastes better than mustard, adds zip to the old bologna." I gave him my best smart-aleck grin.

He gave me a speculative look. "You've got a strange sense of humor," he said.

I patted him on the arm. "Let's just keep it our little secret, okay?"

He walked away then looked back once and banged into some big jock making his way to the exit.

"He's kind of cute," Toni said with a smile.

I didn't take her bait. Instead, I said, "Can you come over to my house today? We could study together."

"That would be great. Mondays are slow. I don't have to work at the market. I really need to catch up on my school stuff."

We agreed to meet at my locker after school.

I was more awake in the afternoon. Funny how time sped up once school was over for the day. It was cool taking the bus with Toni. We talked all the way to my house.

Even that much time together was rare these days. No one was home when we got there, so we had the place to ourselves. I fixed us a snack before we started studying.

"So how's your brother Eddy doing these days?" I asked Toni, remembering her mentioning him at lunch.

"All right, I guess. We don't hear from him much."

"I'm surprised. You'd think he'd be a little bit homesick."

Toni's expressive eyes darkened. "Not for our home he wouldn't."

I viewed her with concern. "Are things bad for you?"

She trained her eyes on the floor. "Yeah, but I don't really want to talk about that. I try never to think of it when I'm not there."

"I didn't know things were so rough is all."

"Let's get some of our work done, okay?"

Not wanting to cause Toni any pain, I dropped it. We set about doing our schoolwork.

Around four, Ailene arrived. She glanced at us glumly, didn't say a word, and quickly went up to her room.

"You're right, she does seem different," Toni observed. "Your sister always used to be so cheerful."

"Yeah, she practically bounced into a room before. Now she just drags along."

"Maybe Jim Saunders is right. Maybe you should talk to her."

"Ailene refers to me as super-pest, and that's when she's in a good mood. No, I somehow don't think I'm the one to talk the talk."

"But then who is?" Toni and I exchanged a look, and I gave her a shrug. That person probably didn't exist.

"Hey, who knows if she really needs anyone's help? Maybe it just isn't anybody's business but hers." That coming from me, of all people, the snoop extraordinaire! But still, it was true.

"Maybe you're right," Toni agreed. "And dating Ray might be very good for her."

"All I know is when he walked in here yesterday, I felt like playing *Born to be Wild* on the stereo system."

Toni giggled, putting her hand over her mouth.

"I'm not joking! They really do rub wrong together. It's like matching Miss America flirt with Rambo."

⌒⌒⌒

Toni and I worked for several hours. By then, my parents got home from work. Dad was very nice to Toni and invited her to stay for dinner.

"Thanks," she said, "but I can't. In fact, it's later than I realized. I really have to get home."

"Well, you and Val can hop into my car, and I'll drive you over."

Toni looked embarrassed. "I don't want to put you to the trouble. I can walk."

"It's too far," I said. It was at least four miles, and it was getting dark. Besides, she would have had to cross the highway to go from Fairview Woods to Crawford's Beach. So Dad and I took Toni home. "I hope you can stay for dinner with us some other time," I told her.

"Maybe," she said, but there was a slight tremor in her voice. "It's really best when I'm there. Otherwise, Kathy has to do the whole meal herself, and she's not ready for it yet. Dad gets upset if it's not done to his liking."

I thought I saw a look of fear momentarily flash across her face. "Does your mom work long hours?"

Toni wouldn't look at me, and when she spoke, her words came haltingly. "My mother doesn't live with us."

I didn't pursue the matter. Anyone could see she was very sensitive on the subject.

"So, how was school today?" my father asked. It was amazing how aware he could be, how he realized just when to discuss something less emotionally charged.

I told Dad about running into Dave Greene in the cafeteria. I didn't tell him about the talk with Jimmy. Toni was quiet and tense during the ride, staring straight ahead. I looked into her eyes, yet had no idea what she was thinking.

We dropped Toni off in front of her house. Actually, it was more like a dilapidated cottage, a few blocks away from the ocean. This entire area had rows of small shanties built on sand. The area had never been very prosperous, and it didn't improve with age. Strange how the highway could separate one part of the township from the other, and how different the character of each area could be when there was so little space between.

Crawford's Beach was one of the old areas. No one swam much at the beach because the water was polluted from the refuse that swept over from Staten Island and the more industrial parts of New Jersey. Of course, that was getting better as industries shut down and moved to other areas. The bad news was they took the jobs with them.

I liked coming to the beach for a walk now and then. It was nice to jog there and breathe the salt air deep into my lungs. It gave me a terrific high. Sometimes I fancied that the point where earth, sea, and sky met must have some religious significance. Such a place seemed holy.

My father drove back to Fairview Woods. Our development bordered a state park on one side, so there was lots of greenery in spring when everything came alive again.

All the houses were middle to upper-middle class, with landscaped lawns and regularly scheduled paint jobs. Rooting out crabgrass was a major obsession. Mother took great pride in having one of the best-maintained lawns in the neighborhood. Dad, on the other hand, was opposed to putting herbicides on the lawn.

Dinner at our house was an exercise in stony silence. No one talked to anyone else. The friendliest it got was when I asked Ailene to pass the ketchup. I don't remember us ever really saying anything important to one another, but this evening even the air was quiet, dinnerware sounds muffled.

It wasn't hard to figure out what was different. Mom wasn't gossiping about anybody or talking to Ailene about clothes shopping. There had always been a closeness between Mom and Ailene, a bonding, because they were so much alike—or at least it seemed that way to me. But now there was a chasm between them, a distance they both seemed to regret. I could tell it was hurting my father too.

"Jimmy asked for you today," I told Ailene, as we were finishing.

"Please don't talk about him," she said in a voice that was much more edgy than necessary.

"Sure, if you say so, but you ought to know that he still cares about you an awful lot. In fact, he's very worried about you."

She jumped to her feet. "There's nothing to worry about." She lifted her chin. "I'm fine, better than I've ever been. I now see clearly." She glanced over at Mother. "I used to live in a world of illusion. I don't anymore." With that, she left the table.

I wondered what she was talking about. I was certain I was missing something. Ailene's words were puzzling.

Mother turned to me. "I wish you hadn't said anything about Jimmy Saunders."

"Why not?"

"You upset Ailene. I think it's obvious he's a thing of the past."

"I disagree. He really does care about her."

My mother smacked her hand against the table. "You always go out of your way to disagree with me, don't you? If I say one thing, you'll say the opposite just for spite."

My father turned to her with a frown. "Jan, I think you misunderstood Val."

Mom's anger was palpable. She rounded on Dad. "And you will always defend her. Some things just do not change." She got up and stalked out like a wet cat, bristly and indignant.

"Sorry," I said to Dad, "didn't mean to cause trouble."

My father sighed. "It's all right. Your mother's on edge. You know she's high-strung, and this thing with Ailene has put her into a terrible mood. You and I will have to be patient until we get this sorted out. We'll have to try to be calm and reasonable and keep out of the argument." Dad wanted to distance himself from the problem and apparently wanted me to join him. It was the way he usually handled things. Mother was more aggressive.

"You really think Mom will be able to find out what's bothering Ailene?"

"I do." There were lines and shadows around my father's eyes that made him look suddenly old and tired. It bothered me a lot to think of him ever aging. I used to think my dad was immortal. One of the bad things about growing up was realizing that no one lives forever.

"I've got to tell you something. Toni knows Ray Zanka, or at least she used to know him. She says he's really a good guy."

"So Toni thinks this fellow is all right?"

"Yeah, Dad, he's cool. So don't worry too much."

"I suppose Ailene might just be going through a stage of adolescent rebellion that will end soon." His eyebrows made that a question.

"I wouldn't know. I'm just a kid myself."

He smiled at me and mussed my hair. "A pretty smart one, I would say."

"You're the only person who thinks so." I leaned over and hugged him. It was really nice hearing a kind word now and then.

I cleaned up the kitchen while Dad went into the family room and read his newspaper. Mom was getting ready to go to her aerobics class.

Ever since she joined this gym, she was spending a lot of her free time there. I was glad. Working out usually puts her in a good mood.

She was already dressed in her tights and shorts, checking for her car keys when the phone rang. Lately, it hadn't been ringing quite so much as usual. I picked it up. The voice at the other end was distinctly masculine, and now familiar.

He asked for Ailene. I called out loudly for her to pick up. When she did, I hung up.

My mother came toward me. "Who was that?"

"Someone for Ailene."

Mother frowned her annoyance at me. "I know that, but who?"

"Some guy," I replied evasively.

"The one from yesterday?"

"I don't know." Well, I didn't know for sure.

She twisted the car keys savagely in her hand. "You do know! But I'm the enemy, aren't I?"

"Stop picking on me."

"You're hardly an abused child. More like a spoiled brat."

Her words cut into me like a knife blade. I gripped a kitchen chair. "There's more than one kind of abuse."

She stood there glaring at me for a moment. "There's also such a thing as parent abuse. People talk about child abuse but forget the abuse a parent suffers from an ungrateful, selfish child."

So she was turning the whole thing around, claiming that I was cruel to her. Well, that really didn't surprise me much. All my life, in one way or another, she'd been telling me I wasn't any good. This was nothing new.

"You know who called Ailene, don't you?"

"Ask her yourself when she gets off the phone."

"I've got to go, or I'll be late for my class. She's been told not to see that vile creature again. She better listen." With that, Mother left, spine stiff, prickly as a porcupine.

I really didn't want to be involved. Dad was right. The best thing was to stay out of it, let Mom and Ailene settle the problem between themselves and keep myself out of the crossfire. Yet knowing I ought to tell Ailene what our mother had said, I went upstairs and waited on the landing. Her voice carried through the door, purring like a cuddly kitten.

After I had waited for what seemed like forever, she still showed no signs of stopping. What could they possibly have to talk about for so long?

For once, I really didn't care to eavesdrop. Ailene was right. I had no life of my own. Why else would I spend so much of my time being nosy about hers? Depression snuck up and attacked me from behind. Was it ever going to change? Would I ever be somebody? Deciding not to wait for Ailene any more, I went to my room.

I turned on the TV in my room and tried to concentrate on some dumb sitcom. At least they had done away with the laugh track, so maybe there was some hope. I realized I would have to talk to Ailene eventually, not for Jimmy, not for Mom, not even for Ailene, but for myself, so I wouldn't have a bad conscience. Even if I hated her guts most of the time, she was still my sister. So, on the commercial break, I knocked on the door to her room.

"Enter," she called out, sounding a lot like I imagined an imperial empress would speak. Regal. Snooty.

"I just wanted to talk to you for a moment. Are you off the phone?"

She nodded. "I bet you couldn't wait to tell Mom and Dad that it was Ray." Her eyes narrowed and shot bullets.

"You always think the worst of me, just like Mom."

"Don't say I'm just like Mom!" She went to her dresser, picked up a brush and began working her hair with a vengeance.

I remembered what Dad had said to me about being calm and reasonable. "I don't want to argue with you."

"Or possibly, you're here to gloat because I'm in trouble with the folks?" She licked her pink upper lip.

"You don't really know me at all. You have no idea what I think or feel."

"Yes, I do. I understand you completely. I know how jealous and vindictive you are. You're a petty, little person."

I stood there staring at her. "I won't deny I've always been envious of you and probably always will be—though I'd like to think someday that'll be different. There's always a girl like you in every school, someone who's gorgeous and athletic and smart, so perfect it makes the rest of us turn green as spring grass. I can accept that. But it really sucks when she's your own sister."

Ailene didn't speak, yet her brushstrokes slowed.

"Believe it or not, I wanted to talk to you because I know something's wrong with you. Jimmy is very concerned too."

She turned and faced me squarely. "I warned you. Don't mention his name again. He's dead to me." Her eyes were like a frozen winter lake, but it occurred to me that this was all on the surface—nothing but a façade—and somewhere in the murky, unexplored depths of Ailene's heart, there was a steaming geyser trapped. It was just a matter of time before the eruption.

"I've got to mention him. You dropping him that way bites. It also doesn't make any sense."

"I won't talk about this with you. You're just one step removed from a diaper change."

I turned on my heels. But then I remembered what Mother said. "Before she left, Mom said you can't go out with Ray again. I think she plans some form of satanic torture if you do."

Her sapphire eyes glittered even brighter, and her pretty face contorted with a sneer. "So I was right all along. This new pose of sisterly concern was all a phony act. You did tell Mom it was Ray who called after all. Just get out of here." She reared back to throw her brush at my head.

I ducked, dashed out, and heard the brush hit the door behind me. I had tried, I told myself, wasn't that enough? But a small voice inside my head said I hadn't done enough.

∽∾∽

On Monday afternoon, I got the school bus driver to let me off on the highway about where I'd walked to after Ailene forced me out of her car on the fateful day when I met the old woman.

I'd taken the music box with me. I wanted to give it back to her and ask her how I could return the wish as well and get my sister back to her normal princess-perfect self.

I found the rural road, but there was no longer a house there. All I saw was construction equipment: backhoes, bulldozers, and shovel diggers. What was going on? I shouted to one of the workers, and he came over and joined me.

"Where's the house and the lady who lives in it?" I asked.

The man removed his hard hat and scratched his bald head. "The property was sold for back taxes to a land developer. He's had us knock everything down. See those corn fields back there? They are going to have a whole development of town houses on them."

"Do you know where the woman is now?"

The construction worker shook his head. "Don't know. I'll ask my boss."

I thanked him and waited while he spoke to his superior. When he returned, he was frowning. I had the worst feeling the news wouldn't be good.

"I'm sorry to tell you that she passed away."

I guess I started to cry without even realizing it because the man placed his hand on my shoulder. "Sorry, kid," he said.

Had the old woman really been a witch? I realized I would never know for certain. I remembered the old saying "God helps those who help themselves." With a deep sigh, I jogged back to the highway.

Chapter 7

Dave Greene tutored me from three to four-thirty on Tuesday afternoon. It was such a beautiful afternoon that I asked if he'd mind sitting out in the yard with me. The yellow-green buds were on the branches of the trees, and the bees were buzzing around the bright yellow forsythia blooms. Everything had been reborn, and it felt good just being alive. It was too nice a day for me to keep my mind on schoolwork. As for Dave, his mind really wasn't on geometry either. He was listless and apparently unable to concentrate. When we finally closed the books for the afternoon, he took off his glasses and rubbed his eyes.

"Tired?" I asked.

"Allergies," he replied. "This weather activates my hay fever. My nose is all clogged." He did sound sort of nasal, but in our part of Central New Jersey, a lot of people do. People say it's caused by their allergies, but I suspect it has a lot to do with air pollution.

"Well, we could go inside for something to drink. Although it does seem a shame when it's so beautiful out here."

"Yes, let's go in," he said, suddenly enthusiastic. When I gave him a surprised look, he added, "I'm just a city boy at heart, I guess."

"I thought all you intellectual types went on and on about the wonders of nature."

He smiled, and I felt the urge to outline his dimple with my finger. "Let's just say I'm more of a scientist than a romantic."

"Even scientists have been known to get romantic at times," I teased.

He hadn't mentioned Ailene all afternoon, and I was feeling pretty good about that.

He followed me through the sliding glass doors and into the family room. "Speaking of getting romantic, how is Ailene doing these days? Does she really intend to go out with that Hell's Angel character?" His tone was casual, but Dave's eyes were intent.

Oh well, nothing good lasts forever. "Truthfully? I don't know. My parents are completely set against it, particularly Mom. With the old Ailene, that would have been enough to end it, but now who knows?"

"So you think she might be seeing him again?"

"Put it this way, Ray called last night, and she talked to him for quite a while. In fact, he's the only person she has been willing to talk to lately."

Dave set his eyes on the carpet. "This isn't going as I expected. Ailene's behavioral deviation from the norm is a lot more complicated than I first imagined."

"Whatever."

He shook his head. "I'm perplexed, but I'm not giving up."

"So you still intend to be my tutor?"

He took out a handkerchief and rubbed his eyeglasses clean. "Naturally. We've got an agreement." He followed me into the kitchen and sat down at the table as I went to the fridge.

I found a six-pack of cola and treated us each to a can. Dave was quiet for a time. He seemed to be working something out in his mind. "There's one thing certain," he finally said after taking a swig of his soda. "She can't go to the prom with a guy like that. It would be too humiliating. She'll have to go with someone normal." There he went, off into fantasyland again.

"I don't know. She's awfully independent lately."

"I know her. Scratch deep enough and there's a social animal under that façade. Ailene isn't going to show up at the ultimate social event with a biker." It sounded like he was trying to convince himself as much as me.

"What if he rents a tux? How can you tell the difference?"

"Are you kidding? There isn't a tux made that would fit over those shoulders."

I nearly choked on my drink. So he had noticed too. "I give up. I'm tired of arguing with you. I'll keep you informed."

"Good. From now on, I'm calling every day."

"Okay." I saluted. "Just be sure to say the secret password, so I know it's really you. I wouldn't want classified information to fall into the wrong hands."

"I don't think I like your attitude," he said slowly.

"Why not?" Our eyes were meeting straight on.

"Because I don't like being mocked."

"Then don't act foolish."

He pulled back from me. "I didn't know I was."

"You are. This whole thing is stupid. Why do you want to go out with a girl who doesn't know you're alive?"

"She knows all right." His myopic eyes registered pain.

"Well, doesn't care then?"

He faced me squarely, his face flushing with color. "Just once, I'd like to be the one everyone admires."

That comment surprised me. "Don't you think you're admired for being as smart as you are?"

"Do you admire me for it?"

We stared at each other. I didn't know how to answer without giving away more than I intended, so he answered it for me. "You don't see me as anything but a brain. If someone's too clever, too good at schoolwork, other kids, the popular ones, in particular, think you're weird. You become a social outcast, a zit on the face of school society."

"So all of this is because you want to be accepted by the popular crowd?"

"I guess when you put it that way, yes, that's exactly what I want."

"Seems to me, you ought to be satisfied with being yourself. There are lots of girls who would appreciate you, like you for yourself, if you gave them a chance. Why don't you ask a girl who would be pleased and proud to be your date to the prom? Forget about Ailene. What's the point of chasing after her? Why go after someone who doesn't care about you?"

Great advice, I thought, why didn't I take it myself? I liked Dave, but he was never going to notice me as anything but his spy.

I was letting my own feelings get trounced, and for nothing. Now I find out that he's not in love with my sister, he just wants her for a trophy!

"You're wrong about Ailene. She's always liked me, but she's never considered me as anything except a casual friend. That's going to change. I'll call you tomorrow."

After he left, I started humming a chorus of "You Don't Know Me," a moldy oldie that fit my mood. I went out back and tried to enjoy the beauty of the spring day by myself. But spring days just naturally awaken a kind of wistful yearning, and it wasn't the same.

ℰᴥℰᴥ

The weekend arrived before I knew it. My parents had plans to visit Mom's sister. Since it was a good distance to North Jersey, near the New York State border, I knew they'd be home late.

"Why don't you both come with us?" Dad said.

"Of course, they're coming," Mother insisted.

"Val should go," Ailene agreed, "but I'm staying home."

Mother was immediately suspicious. "Why don't you want to go?"

Ailene wouldn't look Mom in the eye. "I have other plans."

"What other plans?" Mother was as stubborn as a pit bull with jaws locked.

"Mostly, I have to study for a test. My grades have been slipping lately, and I don't want to finish school with anything less than a B-plus average." Ailene always knew the right thing to say. There was no way Mom could argue with that.

"I suppose it's all right," Mother hesitantly, not really convinced.

"After all, I'm nearly eighteen years old. I'm not a child anymore. You can go away for the evening."

"Ailene's right," Dad said. "She's a young lady now, and we've got to learn to trust her judgment."

I could see Mother was still unsure. "Val will come with us then," she said.

"No way," I replied, "I need to stay home and study too. Toni is coming over on Saturday evening after work. We've got a major paper to write for English." The truth was that, although I disliked Mom's sister's family, I actually did have a lot of schoolwork. It wasn't a total fib.

Ailene was clearly upset by my refusal to go. "You should go," she insisted. "It doesn't look right for both of us not to be there. What will Aunt Sandy think?"

"Who cares?" I said.

My mother gave me a reproving look.

"I wish I could claim homework as an excuse not to go," Dad said with a grin.

"You're all terrible," Mother exclaimed.

It took a few more minutes of convincing, but in the end, she accepted that we would not be going with her.

About half a minute after my parents were on the road, Ailene rushed to her room and shut the door. I had a suspicion, so I carefully lifted the telephone receiver. Sure enough, she was busy dialing.

"Get off, you little snoop!" she shouted as the ringing sounded.

I dropped the receiver. When I picked it up again a few minutes later, all I got was a dial tone. But I was certain I knew who she had called anyway. And it turned out I was right.

At two o'clock in the afternoon, Ray Zanka showed up at our door. Ailene had apparently been watching for him because when he knocked, she came flying down the stairs, something I'd never seen her do for any other guy. She tried to steer him away before I could see who it was.

"I know it's Ray, so don't bother to hide him on my account. You can ask him in."

Ailene stuck her tongue out at me. I made a childish face back at her. So much for maturity.

"Ray, would you like to come in? I have to talk to my sister for just a minute."

"Sure," he said with a good-natured smile. "No hurry, I've finished working for today. I got the whole afternoon free."

Ailene grabbed my arm none too gently and steered me into the kitchen. "You are pond slime," she said.

"Thank you, I simply adore your compliments," I simpered.

She gave me a shove, and I shoved her back.

"You're not going to tell Mom or Dad that I'm seeing Ray. Is that understood?" Her voice was menacing, and I felt a surge of anger.

"Save your threats because there's nothing you can do to me. You may be bigger than I am, but I can protect myself. Anyway, maybe Mom and Dad should know what a sneak you've turned into."

"Ha! You, calling me a sneak? That's rich." Her face was almost as pink as her nail polish. She wasn't half as attractive when she was sneering.

"I wasn't going to tell our folks anything." I hated the way her eyes squinted when she was angry. My words sounded sullen, even to me.

"I don't believe you."

"Then maybe I should tell them."

Ray came into the kitchen. "Private chick party?"

"Not at all." Ailene fixed a phony smile on her lips before she turned to face him. "I'm ready to go shopping with you anytime."

"Shop 'til you drop," I said.

"Maybe the kid would like to come along," he suggested. His dark eyes twinkled at me.

"Where you going?" I asked.

"Out to get your sister the kind of clothes she needs if she's going to hang out with me."

"Sounds interesting. Sure, I'd love to come along."

"Absolutely not! You have homework to do. Remember?"

"Well, maybe I'll just stay home and call Mom and Dad. See if they're at Aunt Sandy's yet." I gave her my best cat-that-just-ate-the-canary look. I figured she deserved it.

Her face flushed scarlet. "Oh, all right. I guess you can come along, but don't make too much of a nuisance of yourself."

I almost laughed out loud. Revenge was sweet.

They couldn't take Ray's motorcycle because I was coming along. Ailene hadn't ridden on it yet, and I think in spite of her protests, she was relieved to take her own car. Still, she did offer to let Ray drive.

"It's your car," he said.

"No, I really want you to drive. Besides, you know where we're going, and I don't."

So Ray ended up driving with all three of us squeezed into the front of the Corvette. I was hugging the door, sharing a seat with Ailene, and being very grateful I was so skinny.

Ray surprised me by being a careful, courteous driver. It wasn't what I expected. However, the place where he took us was exactly what I did expect. It was in one of those sleazy flea markets that open only on weekends. Ailene, who always shopped in malls and fancy boutiques, looked a little shocked by the atmosphere, but she did a fair job of hiding it from Ray.

As for me, I was fascinated. There seemed to be an in-

ordinate number of cutpurses lurking around, but one
look at Ray and they steered clear of us.

Ray steered us to a store with the logo "Low-cost
Leathers." He found a rack of black leather jackets for
women and had Ailene start trying them on. She took her
sweet time making a choice. Finally, she found one that
fit to her satisfaction.

"What do you think?" Ray asked me.

"All you need now are chains and a whip. Then Ailene
will be perfectly accessorized."

My sister threw me a dirty look, and Ray tried to hide
his irritation. He didn't move, just flexed.

"Just joking," I said. "It looks totally cool. A perfect
fit." I rolled my eyes, though. The sight of her in a motorcycle jacket was kind of weird.

"Well, I think this jacket looks great on me," Ailene
said with a proud tilt of her head. "I'm going to take it."

Ray relaxed and flashed a smile that would have done
any male model proud. "Great, I'll pay for it."

Ailene looked surprised. "Absolutely not! It's my
jacket. I'll pay."

"But you're buying it to wear on my bike."

"I have my birthday money. Dad told me to bank it,
but mother said that I should buy something I wanted
with it. Well, up until now, I didn't know what to buy.
Now I do."

There was no arguing with Ailene when she made up
her mind about something. She was as stubborn as Mom.
So she bought the jacket and a pair of matching tight

leather pants that only took half a lifetime to pick out, and she seemed happy enough.

While we were waiting for Ailene to check out, Ray turned to me. "So I don't think you like me very much. Why is that, kid?" He knit his dark, bushy brows and his ebony eyes bore into mine.

I met his gaze as directly as I could with my neck craning to look up at him. "First off, I hate being called *kid*. My name is Val. It's real easy to remember. Second, you're not the type of guy Ailene would normally date if she were in her right mind, so I have to wonder where this is going."

"And that worries you, *Val*?" He emphasized my name.

"Yeah, it does. My whole family is in an uproar."

"Just the same, this is a free country. Your sister seems to want to go out with me. I'm not holding a gun on her. See?" He raised his hands, palm up. What I saw were the calluses of a working man's hand. "Just keep your mind open, okay?"

"It's not important what I think anyway, is it?"

He shrugged. "I didn't say that."

"I don't care one way or the other who Ailene dates. I've got nothing against you personally."

"Okay, glad to hear it."

"But I guess it's only fair to warn you, my parents don't approve of you, and it's not likely they ever will."

"We'll just have to see how this plays out," Ray said thoughtfully.

After that important bit of shopping was over, and we were back on the road, Ray stopped at the local mall and insisted on treating us to ice cream at Ralph's. We each chose a different ice cream creation, and I have to admit, I had fun in spite of myself. Most of that was Ray's doing. He wouldn't allow me to feel like a third wheel, which was what I had expected, especially after the little scene in the leather shop.

We walked in the mall for a while, until Ray led us into the arcade. We all played a few video games, but Ray's specialty was pinball. I drifted away from them, trying various video games while Ray and Ailene worked on a pinball machine together. It apparently involved a lot of handholding.

We got back to the house just before Toni was due to arrive. Ailene invited Ray in, and he agreed to stay. They went into the rec room, and she put on the stereo. She chose Madonna's latest album and started dancing around the room, modeling her new jacket. Ray watched her for a few minutes. Then he got up and took off his leather jacket, his biceps bulging beneath his T-shirt. He took Ailene's soft, milk-white hand in his big, callused one, drew her into his arms, and they began to slow dance. She put her head on his shoulder, and he held her very close.

It made me feel funny inside watching how they were together. I very quietly left the room, wondering if any guy would ever look at me that way.

Going outside to wait for Toni, I stared at our well-manicured lawn. No dandelions were allowed here. Every blade of grass had a proper pedigree. I was getting impatient for Toni to arrive. She would probably take the bus across town from the civic center. That should leave her only a few blocks from the house.

At last, I saw her walking up the block. I jogged over to meet her, and we walked back together. The day's warmth and the exercise had created beads of moisture on her tired face. Then I noticed the bruises, two large black and blue marks on the right side of her face, and her lower lip was split and slightly swollen.

"What happened to your face?"

She flushed. "Some people at work asked me that today too. It's nothing. I'm clumsy. I slipped and fell in the house yesterday evening."

I had the feeling that wasn't the truth.

"Let me get you a cold drink. I guess you had a long, hot walk."

"Not so bad," she said, her eyelids fluttering like butterflies in flight, trying to avoid looking me in the eye.

When we got inside, I called out to Ailene that Toni had arrived. I didn't want to go anywhere near the rec room, or she would think that I was spying on them.

Ailene and Ray came into the kitchen while I got Toni a glass of juice.

"Would you like anything?" Ailene asked him.

"I've already got what I want," he said with a teasing smile. "Will you let me take you for a ride on my bike? That way you can try out your new jacket."

She gave him a flirty smile. "I guess so."

"Good, then let me take you out to a movie this evening."

"I'd like to see *The Breakfast Club*."

"Sounds like a chick flick," he said. "But sure, whatever you want."

"I'll just go upstairs and change," Ailene said in a saccharine voice. She turned to me and said, just as sweetly, "Be a good hostess while I'm gone. Don't make any rude remarks to Ray." Her eyes had a completely different tone.

"Ailene thinks I have no manners," I explained as my sister left the kitchen.

"Is she right?" he asked with an easy smile.

"Of course, I'm a real pain, just ask anyone."

"No, she's not," Toni said in a shy voice.

"You've got to be her loyal friend—Don't I know you?"

"I'm Eddy Walker's sister."

He smiled warmly. "Sure, I remember! How's Eddy doing?"

"Okay, I guess," Toni replied, in a barely audible voice.

"Remember me to him, when you see him next time."

I got Ray and myself each a can of cola while Toni sipped her juice, and then we all sat down at the kitchen table.

The golden rays of the late afternoon sun shining through the kitchen window made the room bright and cheerful. It also provided excellent lighting for the injured side of Toni's face.

Ray got a glimpse of the bruises and gently turned her head so he could see them better. "Wow! That looks nasty. Val, you got any ice?"

"Sure thing," I said, going over to the freezer. I cracked out some ice, took a clean towel, and wrapped it around. "How's that for an ice pack?"

I could tell Toni was terribly embarrassed. "Please, you shouldn't have bothered. This is nothing." She tried to push it away, but Ray picked up the ice pack and pressed it against her face. She looked so fragile and vulnerable.

"Stay still," he said, holding her shoulder with his other hand.

"I—I don't need any help with this." She pulled away from him. Her lower lip trembled, and I thought that she was about to cry. She wouldn't look at either of us.

"Take it easy," I said while rubbing small circles on the middle of her back. Ray and I exchanged a concerned look over the top of her head.

"Say, how long do you think Ailene's going to take?" he said, to change the subject.

"The princess likes to primp before making an entrance. My guess is that we should probably go into the rec room and turn on the TV. There might be something good on cable."

Ray and Toni followed me into the other room. Finding nothing worth watching, I just tuned the stereo to some pop and rock, and we sat back and relaxed.

"Do you still live at the beach?" Ray asked Toni.

She nodded her head. "Do you?"

"No, not since I left school."

I was reminded of what Jimmy had told us about Ray. My curiosity was getting the better of me again.

"Ray, Did you drop out of Wilson your senior year?"

"Yeah, I did." His depthless eyes were suddenly so dark they made me shiver.

"I was thinking of doing that when I turn sixteen," Toni blurted.

All I could do was stare at her in surprise. "How can you even consider that?" I asked.

"I might have to do it for my family."

I shook my head, unable to fathom what kind of family would make such cruel demands of its children.

"In a way, I did it because of my family, too," Ray said. He took a long swallow from his can of cola. His Adam's apple bobbed.

"Your parents needed you to work?" Toni asked, her large eyes intent on him.

"Not exactly. My old man booted my ass out."

I guess I just stared again. "Why would he do a thing like that?"

"Because I tried to interfere when he smacked my mother around."

I started to choke on my soda and had to put it down.

He reached over and tapped me the back. "Hey, you all right, kid?"

"Fine," I replied, still coughing, "it just went down the wrong way."

"Shocked you, didn't I?" His smile was knowing, but his voice was flat and emotionless.

"No, I was just surprised."

"I didn't think parents threw kids out." Toni's soft, delicate voice sounded pensive. "I thought kids were like

Eddy. They just sort of got away as soon as they could if things were bad at home."

I recognized that Toni realized she'd said more than she meant to because she cast her eyes on the floor and her cheeks flushed.

"You'd be surprised how many kids don't run away, they get thrown away. Anyhow, that was what happened to me."

"Your dad really used to hit your mom?" I asked.

"Whenever things didn't go right for him, and that was a lot of the time. He seemed to need to take his frustrations out on somebody, and she was convenient. Of course, she didn't help matters any because she wouldn't stand up for herself. She just kept taking it, let him use her for a punching bag. I was the oldest, so I was more aware of it than anyone else. I told her she should leave him, but she kept saying she didn't have anywhere to go, that she couldn't support herself and us. So she stayed, and she always made excuses for him. It made me so mad." Ray crushed his empty soda can.

"Did he hit you?" Toni asked.

His eyes met hers. "Only when I got in the way and tried to stop him from touching her. He left my two little sisters alone entirely, thank God!" He stood up and began pacing the room. "I started working part-time at a garage when I was about your age. I figured if I earned enough money, I could give it to her, and it might convince her to leave him. But she just wouldn't go.

"Anyway, by the time I was seventeen, I was pretty big. I'd been working out with weights regularly. Almost never lost a wrestling match. Finally figured I might be able to take my old man on. So the next time he started working her over, I decked him. He got off the floor and he just stared at me. My old man is a big guy, bigger than me.

"He's in construction and keeps fit. So he said we'd take it outside, and I said that was just fine by me. My mother and sisters were crying, but we ignored them. We had quite a battle, him and me. But he eventually beat me. When he did, he said that was it. He wanted me out. 'Never come back,' he said. Then he called me a few things I wouldn't repeat in front of you innocent young ladies."

"You had to leave school?" Toni's face was full of sympathy.

"There wasn't any choice. I stayed with a friend for a few days, but I had to find a place of my own. That takes money. Sam Harper took me on full-time when I explained my situation to him. He's all right, a stand-up guy. He said he was glad to have me because I'd been doing good work for him, and he needed more help anyway since business was improving. I've been working for him ever since. He's taught me a lot. I'm a decent mechanic, thanks to him."

"But you really should have at least a high school diploma," I said.

"Sure, I agree. One of these days, I'll finish up."

"What about night school? You could get your equivalency there. It might open a few doors for you career-wise."

Ray smiled at me, as if seeing me for the first time. "You're okay, Val. You got your head on straight. Yeah, I'll do it soon. I'd like to train to fix those expensive foreign jobs like Mercedes. Sam's a good boss, but I'd like to move up, maybe someday own my own garage."

"It's great you've got ambition." Toni eyed him with admiration.

"What happened with your family?" I asked Ray.

"Nothing very good. About eight months ago, my mother died." There was no mistaking the pain in his eyes. He sat down heavily on the sofa as if punched.

"I'm really sorry," I murmured.

"Oh, they said it was an accident, but I knew different. She didn't fall down a flight of stairs. He probably pushed her. But nobody believed me. The cops said there wasn't any proof. I know the truth, though."

I had an alarming thought. "Your sisters, are they still with him?"

"No, Mom's parents came in from Pennsylvania when she died. They took charge of my sisters. It's good, knowing they're safe. The old man didn't really want them anyway. He was never meant to care for children. I don't even know where he is now. He just took off. Good riddance!" Flashing eyes and clenched fists gave evidence of the rage he had built up thinking about dear old dad. He was having some difficulty sitting still and was now on the edge of his seat. "Someday, maybe I'll meet up with him again. I've been building myself up for it. Only this time, he won't win." He finished squashing the soda can still in his hand and then set it down on the end table.

"I hope you never see him again," I said. "You'll probably just destroy your life if you do."

"I understand how Ray feels," Toni said with surprising vehemence. "My parents always used to argue. One day, my mother just walked away and left us. And that's when everything got so bad."

"I'm back," Ailene said, standing in the doorway.

The intensity of the confessional was shattered—just when Toni was about to open up and tell us what was going on with her. I could have screamed in frustration.

Chapter 8

You all look terribly somber. What have you been talking about since I left?"

Ailene posed like a model. Designer jeans accentuated the perfection of her slender figure. She was wearing that pink silk blouse that I had admired in her closet. It fit her really well, I noticed, feeling more than a tad jealous. Her make-up was flawless, every hair in place.

"Ain't no sunshine when you're not around," Ray said with an appreciative smile. He put his hands around her tiny waist and lifted her up in the air.

"Ray, put me down!" she squealed. She pummeled his rippling shoulders with her fists, and he carefully lowered her. "How did you ever build such powerful muscles?" she asked with a flirtatious smile.

"Oh, I pick up cars and put them on the lift to fix. It's great exercise." His eyes twinkled with laughter.

She pummeled him again. "No, really."

"Been weightlifting for years now. I take karate at a school with great facilities, and for a small extra fee I can use the gym at the dojo."

Toni's eyes opened wide. "Do you split boards and stuff like that?"

Ray laughed. "That's only part of it, but yeah, we do that. Mostly, it's learning self-defense and good mental attitudes, confidence-building."

"I can't imagine anyone starting a fight with you." I was only stating the obvious.

He smiled at me in that good-natured way he had. "You'd be surprised. Sometimes when you look tough, guys start with you for no good reason."

"Think maybe they don't feel good about themselves?" I asked.

"Could be," Ray agreed.

While we were talking, the phone began to ring. Ailene went to answer it. After several minutes, she called out for me to pick up. It was Mom, saying they would be delayed and probably wouldn't arrive home before midnight. She asked if everything were all right in such a way, I knew exactly what she really meant. I hesitated before responding.

"Everything's fine here."

"And Ailene, what's she doing?"

I really hated to lie, but I rationalized it was in a good cause. Besides, I really didn't want to tell Mom about

Ray. "Ailene's doing her homework and painting her toenails, in that order."

Mother breathed a sigh of relief. "All right, take care. Don't forget to have a decent dinner. There's a casserole in the refrigerator that you can heat up."

I thanked her and quickly hung up. Now my conscience was stinging me. Yet I hadn't been able to tell her that Ray was here. In truth, once you got to know him, he was okay. He had his head on straight, except maybe for wanting to murder his father. But that was understandable.

"Everything all right?" Ailene asked me pointedly.

"I told Mom and Dad you were studying. Why don't you and Ray hang out with us? Mom left a casserole for dinner. I can nuke it."

Ailene looked annoyed. "I've already got a mother, if you'll remember. Come on, Ray, let's get going."

"Sure, whatever you like, beautiful."

"I'll get my new jacket. This seems like a perfect evening to take a ride on your bike."

Ray looked pleased. His eyes followed Ailene as she left the room. "Your sister is really something," he said in admiration.

I kept my mouth shut because I didn't see Ailene in quite the same light Ray did. My mouth could have rolled over her like a tank. I was more than a little irked that she put me in the position of having to lie for her, without showing the slightest drop of gratitude for the way I covered for her. If gratitude was rain, I'd be living in Death Valley.

"Hey, you two take it easy while we're gone. Put a little more ice on that cheek," he said to Toni. "It's too pretty a face to be beat up that way." He put one arm around Toni and the other around me. "It's been good talking to you. In fact, I think this is the most talking I've ever done about myself. You're good company, both of you."

Ailene returned in her black leather jacket. "What's this? Are you charming all the younger girls, too?" Toni pulled away, looking embarrassed. "I just can't turn my back on you for a second," Ailene teased.

Ray smiled at her. "I only date one beautiful girl at a time."

"You're sure I can trust you?" She was all full of exaggerated play-suspicion, but the way she hung on his arm branded it flirting.

"Now, I never said that," he teased back. Ray picked up his own jacket and slung it across his shoulder.

"Don't wait up," Ailene called back.

After they were gone, Toni and I started to do some schoolwork, except Toni seemed distracted. Her mind just wasn't on writing term papers. I wondered if she was thinking about Ray or maybe whatever had caused her bruises.

Toni wasn't going to open up to me, I could see that. She had come the closest to it when Ray was with us. He seemed to have the ability to bring Toni out of herself. Now she was withdrawn again, barely speaking. Whenever her mind wandered, her violet eyes took on a sad, troubled expression.

I wanted to help her but I didn't know how. I was out of my depth, and I knew it.

We broke for dinner around seven o'clock. Just as I started to heat the casserole, the doorbell rang, and rang again before I could get there.

"Who's there?" I called out. I really wasn't expecting anyone, and I doubted Ailene would return this early.

"It's Dave Greene," a stilted voice called back.

I opened the door. "Had dinner yet?"

"A while ago, why?"

"I was going to invite you to eat with us."

"I could manage something," he said with an eager smile. He followed me quickly to the kitchen, then looked around disappointedly. "Where's Ailene and your parents?"

"They're all out. But you can have Toni and me for company." I studied his crestfallen expression. "Gee, I hope you won't start jumping up and down. Big displays of enthusiasm make me nervous."

He looked over at Toni. "Wow, that's some bruise you got there! Who hit you?"

Toni's head drooped like a willow tree ready to weep. She got to her feet unsteadily. "Excuse me for a moment," she said. "I better call my sister and see if she's okay. Can I use the phone in the other room?"

"Of course." I waited until Toni left and then I spun around to face Dave. "How could you be so insensitive?"

He gave me a bewildered look. "What are you talking about?"

"You mean to say that you really don't know?" I shook my head in disbelief. "How can such a smart guy be so dumb?"

"Don't ride me tonight, okay?" he said irritably. "I'm getting sick of your acid tongue. Who are you anyway?"

I pushed him hard, and he lost his balance, ending up on the floor. He looked so silly sprawled on the kitchen floor that I began to giggle. Suddenly, he was laughing with me. I offered him a hand to help him up. He took it and pulled me down next to him.

We were looking into each other's eyes. I wasn't laughing anymore, and neither was he. His face was flushed. For just a moment, I thought he was going to kiss me, and my heart started to beat excitedly. I moved toward him.

Then he quickly pulled back, as if he'd caught himself making a mistake.

"Is this part of some plan to make me look like even a bigger jerk," he accused.

I was instantly angry again. "I don't have to make you do anything. You manage to act like a dummy all by yourself."

"You really dislike me, don't you?"

"Think whatever you like," I replied, picking myself off the marble tile and brushing myself off.

He rose stiffly to his feet. "Guess I saw through that all right," he said uncertainly.

"Yeah, I guess you're a real genius. Maybe you should change your name to Einstein."

I stalked back to the stove to check the casserole. It was already hot. I sprinkled a little Parmesan cheese over the casserole and put it back in the oven until Toni returned. I started chopping up a salad with vigor.

Dave watched me, his thin arms folded across his chest. "What did that lettuce ever do to you? You're practically decapitating it."

"I was pretending it was your head."

Our hostilities were interrupted by Toni's return. I was glad to have her back.

"How's your sister?" I asked.

"Kathy's fine, but I ought to be getting home soon."

"I was hoping you might sleep over tonight," I said, feeling a sense of disappointment.

Her eyes were lowered. "Wish I could, but I can't leave Kathy alone."

"Your Dad's home, isn't he?"

Toni bit her lower lip. "Might be there, might not, but she's only ten. It's best if I'm there at night."

"Okay, first we have dinner. I'll make it quick. Dave, how did you get over here?"

"Borrowed Mom's car."

"Great! Then you can give Toni a ride home."

"Thought I'd hang out here for a while," he protested.

"Ailene won't be back right away. She can't be out too late because our folks expect her to be home when they arrive. So, if you take Toni home, you can come back and hang out 'til she arrives."

"No," Toni said, "I walked here, and there's no reason I can't walk back."

"Absolutely not," I told her, dishing out whatever it was Mom had put in the casserole.

"This macaroni and cheese doesn't taste right," Dave complained, after the first couple of bites.

I handed him the Parmesan. "Here, sprinkle more of this on. It'll help. My mom is into health food. That means substitutes for everything—like tofu mixed with yogurt." Prisoners eating their final meal before execution have probably chewed with more enthusiasm. "It's nutritious, even if it doesn't taste good."

"That's what my mother always says about broccoli, but I don't like it either."

The meal ended on a quiet note. Toni helped me clean and stack the dishes in the dishwasher. Then she got ready to leave. I elbowed Dave as she was going toward the door.

"Wait up," he said, checking each of his pockets until he finally came up with the car keys.

"I don't feel right about this," Toni said.

"No, it's okay, really," Dave said. "I agree with Val, you shouldn't walk alone that far and this late. Probably it's the only thing she and I will ever agree about."

"I'll come along," I told her. "It's a nice evening for a drive. I'd like to get out for a while."

So off we went—after a few minutes, anyway. Dave was kind of nervous behind the wheel. For a while, I wasn't certain we'd ever make it out of my driveway, much less to Crawford's Beach.

"Do you want us to come in or anything?" I asked as we finally drove up to Toni's house.

"Oh, no," she quickly replied. "Thanks for everything. I'll see you in school on Monday."

We waved goodbye to her, watching her slim figure disappear into the dilapidated bungalow. In all the time I knew her, Toni had never invited me into her house.

"I didn't know Toni lived in Crawford's Beach," Dave said.

"Well, where did you think she lived?"

"I don't know, just somewhere else, maybe somewhere nicer, I suppose. She's really a sweet kid. Most of the burn-outs at school come from this area."

"Now you know why you can't stereotype people."

He viewed me out of the corner of his eye. "Thank you for the sermon."

"Sorry, didn't know I'd given one."

"I'll drive you home," he said, his expression wooden.

"Would you like to take a walk along the beach first?" I ventured. "I mean, as long as we're here."

He looked around doubtfully. "Is it safe in this part of town?"

"Sure, why not? It's a public beach, isn't it?"

He cut across to the beachfront parking area. We left the locked car and headed over to the small boardwalk, deserted at this time. Gossamer wisps of clouds moved across a gibbous moon above us.

"I can see the North Star," I said pointing. "Look how brilliant it is."

"Great visibility from here," Dave observed. "You can see all the way to Staten Island. See that bridge?"

It must have been high tide because the surf came up as I walked along the water line and caught me unawares.

"Oh no! My sneakers are wet."

He started to laugh. "Now who's the dork?"

I gave him a hard shove, trying to push him toward the

water. He shoved me back in the other direction. We both ended up off balance and fell on the sand. "Are you deliberately trying to keep me in a horizontal position?" he teased.

"I just don't want you being too sure of yourself," I told him.

"You don't have much to fear in that regard."

I brushed myself off and ran down the beach.

"Wait," he called after me. "Don't go running off in the dark."

I stopped and turned around. "Okay, if you promise to go jogging with me this week."

He grimaced. "I hate unnecessary physical activity."

"It's good for your body and your mind. Helps create self-discipline. Besides, Ailene likes athletes, remember? And anybody can jog."

He finally agreed, making sure I knew it was under protest, and we set Tuesday afternoon as Dave's date with destiny.

He took my hand as we walked to the car.

"How nice, you're holding my hand," I said with a touch of sarcasm.

"I just want to make sure you don't run off again. You're pretty unpredictable."

"Don't worry. I won't leave you alone in the dark."

"Tell me, how is it that you've lived this long without someone cutting out your tongue?"

"It's been tried. How do you think I got to be such a fast runner?"

That made him smile, and when he did, I could see the

shadow of his dimple in the moonlight. I sighed and wished I were Ailene. Dave, Jimmy, and Ray all wanted to be with her. Every guy wanted Ailene. Nobody wanted me.

We got in the car and, thinking of the last trip, I fastened my seat belt. After one false start, which featured him jamming on his brakes before we got onto the highway and me being grateful for the seat belt, Dave finally got us back to my house.

When he shut off the ignition, Dave turned to me. "Val," he said, "I've got something important to ask you. And don't make fun of me because this is a serious matter."

My ears perked up. Had he changed his mind about Ailene? Did he realize how much better I would be for him?

"Your friend, Toni, is she an abused child?"

I just sat there staring at him. "I—I don't know."

His eyes met mine, and he looked genuinely concerned. "But you think that, don't you?"

I was pensive for a time. "She really doesn't want to discuss it with me. I don't feel it's my place to butt in."

He took my hand distractedly. "Don't you think you should at least try to talk to her about it, offer to help, or something?"

"I guess you're right," I said. "I'll talk to her Monday. I take it back. You are sensitive."

"For a dork?" He laughed then, and it surprised me because I never realized before that he had any sense of humor.

Maybe I had been too hard on him. "I'm the jerk," I said.

"No, you're okay." He surprised me then by leaning over and kissing my cheek. "Think we can call a truce and be friends?"

I wanted to tell him that I didn't think of him as a friend, but I realized that friendship was better than nothing. "Sure," I said. "You can never have too many friends."

We went back into the house, and I was glad to have Dave with me. At night, the house was large, empty, and just a little spooky. I quickly put on most of the downstairs lights. "My dad has some good ice cream stashed in the freezer. Want some? It's maple walnut."

"I'm partial to chocolate chip, but when it comes to ice cream I'm not really picky," he said smiling.

He followed me to the kitchen, and I scooped out two bowls of maple walnut ice cream, a large one for him and a small one for me.

"What do you think of Einstein's theory of relativity?" I asked.

He started to laugh. "I thought you weren't going to mock on me anymore."

"I was being serious," I said with some indignation. "I figured that's the kind of stuff you liked talking about."

We didn't get any further in our discussion because at that moment, I heard someone at the front door.

"Ailene?" he asked eagerly. His face lit up like a TV screen. He might as well have stuck a knife in me.

I followed as he hurried toward the front hall. Sure

enough, Ailene strolled in, followed by Ray. The look on Dave's face as he caught sight of Ailene made my heart hurt.

"What an experience! It's really something riding on a motorcycle." She and Ray exchanged a smile. "Totally exhilarating."

This was the first time I could ever remember seeing her hair messed up.

"We were just having ice cream in the kitchen. Care to join us?"

"I already had enough of that for one day. And so did you."

"I'll jog it off tomorrow," I said.

We left Ailene to say goodnight to Ray. It was obvious, to me, at least, that they wanted to be alone. I practically had to drag Dave out of the hall.

When Ailene came into the kitchen, she was by herself. We could hear the bike pulling out.

"Have a good time?" I asked her.

She answered with a big smile. Dave looked less than happy.

"I didn't know you and Val were getting together tonight," she said to him.

"Dave really came over to see you," I said.

"Me? What did you want to see me about?" Ailene's bright, blue eyes opened wide in surprise.

"I think he has something to ask you."

Ailene was staring at him, rosebud lips slightly parted. "What was it you wanted to ask me, Dave?"

Dave's face colored deeply. He couldn't seem to tear his eyes away from her mouth. He looked relieved when the sound of a car pulling into the driveway diverted Ailene's attention.

Chapter 9

Ailene turned to me and then to Dave. "The folks can't know I was out tonight."

"You can depend on me," Dave promised her.

Ailene literally flew to the front door to greet Mom and Dad.

Dave grabbed my arm angrily. "What was that about? You know I wasn't ready to ask her to the prom yet. It's not the right time. I thought I could trust you. Some friend!"

I yanked my arm free and walked by him. I didn't say anything. How could I tell him how much it pained me to see the way he looked at Ailene? How I wished just once he would look at me that way.

My mother came toward Dave. "It was so nice of you to come by and spend time with the girls this evening. It makes me feel so much better knowing Ailene has a friend like you. I hope you realize that you're always welcome here."

Dave blushed slightly.

"Mother, you're embarrassing him," Ailene said. Her brows arched in disapproval.

"That's all right," Dave quickly responded. He turned to Mother. "Thank you for the invitation. I appreciate it, but right now I need to get going. See you folks." He left then, looking pleased and content.

Ailene and I followed our parents into the recreation room. Mother put down her handbag and smiled at both of us. "It's nice to know that your father and I can go out and not have to worry about your welfare," she said.

Dad put his arm around her shoulders. "I told you that, but you didn't believe me. Our girls are almost grown up now. We can trust them to do the right thing."

I fixed my eyes on the carpet and bit my lower lip feeling guilty. However, Ailene had to be the one to tell our parents the truth about this evening, not me.

"You're home earlier than we expected," Ailene said.

"Your father was eager to get back. Personally, I would have slept over if the two of you had come with us."

"Thank God we didn't," I said.

"They only say nice things about you," Mother asserted.

I rolled my eyes. "What they say and what they mean are two different things."

"Well, I'm glad to be home," Dad said with a yawn. "I'm not in your brother-in-law's league, financially, and

I don't care to be constantly reminded of it."

I knew exactly what my father was talking about. Aunt Sandy and Uncle Robert were obscenely wealthy. They had full-time servants and lived in a mansion. Aunt Sandy didn't work like Mom. Instead, she was a dilettante who volunteered time for charity when she got bored. It was beneath her to earn a paycheck.

She graciously deigned to help the less fortunate by working free for charitable organizations, thereby removing a chance to earn a paycheck by some ordinary slob. Our aunt lived an entirely different life style, one that Mother envied.

I looked at my parents thoughtfully. They made an attractive couple. Mom had dressed up in her finest for the visit, wearing her best jewelry. Dad's dark brown hair made a nice contrast to her fairness. Silver had begun to salt his temples. I thought it made him look distinguished.

"Were there any messages? Did anyone drop by?"

"No messages, and Toni was by earlier."

Mother frowned. "I wish you'd make some friends with girls who live around here."

"I already know you don't approve of Toni."

"She's a sweet child, but hardly the right sort of person for you."

"Who would be better? Some stuck-up snob that you pick?"

My mother started to look angry.

Dad, catching it, stepped between us. "We're all tired now. Let's just relax, shall we? How about we go into the kitchen and have some dessert?"

"I'll fix it for you," I told him.

"None for me," Mother said, raising her hand, as if to ward off the calories.

The phone rang. Ailene rushed to answer it. She returned a few moments later.

"It's for me. I'll take it in my room. Val, hang up the phone down here when I tell you."

I gave a solemn nod. "Yes, she who must be obeyed."

I did as Ailene commanded. Mother frowned at me when I returned. I guess she hadn't missed Ailene's air of secrecy even if it was discreet. Mother excused herself and also went upstairs. That left Dad and me alone, which was just as well. By tacit agreement, we went to the kitchen. He turned to me as I was dishing out ice cream for him. "How did it go tonight?" His quiet question set off my alarms.

"I thought we already told you." I concentrated on the bowl, placing scoops of ice cream precisely.

"You told us what you knew we wanted to hear."

I shifted my weight uneasily from one foot to the other. "Dad, please don't pressure me. I'm not free to answer you."

"I wish you felt you could trust me," he said, furrowing his brow.

I lowered my eyes. "If it were just me, I would." I handed him the ice cream, but he only sat there staring at it.

"Suddenly, I don't feel much like dessert. Save it for another time when there's something to celebrate." He pushed the dish away and left the room.

Tears leaked out while I planned Ailene's gruesome murder in my head. She always got away with everything, and here I was, put in this awful spot because of her. And all I got from her in return was more misery. I dumped the ice cream in the sink and rinsed the bowl.

They had all gone upstairs, which I thought a good thing. Sometimes, a person was better off being alone.

I turned on the big television set in the family room and flipped through the remote to the major cable stations just to see if there were any interesting movies on. Seemed like the more channels they added, the less of interest there was to watch. I settled on a chick flick mindless enough to make me feel better. I wanted to turn off my brain, end the thinking, and above all, the guilt.

I must have fallen asleep there because when I woke up, I was shivering on the couch and there was a bad taste in my mouth.

It was still dark, so I made my way upstairs, brushed my teeth and then fell into my bed. I didn't wake up again until I heard the birds trilling to each other in the trees.

Someone was already up. It was early on Sunday morning, and I didn't feel much like getting out of bed, but the smell of food cooking made my stomach growl. It was hopeless. I had to have something to eat. I found my father at the kitchen stove.

"Where's Mom?"

"Still in bed. I decided to serve her this morning. I'll do the cooking, and you can serve."

"As long as I get the first batch of pancakes," I told

him. He had made my favorite kind with fresh strawber-
ries and cream on top.

"These are crepes," he said.

"I'm taking Spanish, not French," I told him.

"Well, if your mother asks, they're crepes. She doesn't
eat pancakes." He gave me a wink.

After plowing my way through a generous helping, I
took a tray up to Mom. I knocked at the door and she said
to come in. She was listening to the radio. I set down the
tray beside her. Dad had even put a red rose from the
garden beside her coffee and juice.

"Looks delicious, but terribly fattening. I hope your
father won't eat too many of these." I didn't answer, leaving quietly.

Dad was glancing at the sports page when I returned to
the kitchen.

"Anything interesting happening in the world?"

Dad shrugged. "There's always something happening
somewhere. Some of it pretty terrible. But I'd say President Reagan's been doing a good job for us in our country."

It promised to be a quiet day, a family-ritual-type
Sunday with all of us sitting around reading the newspaper in the morning and then each more or less doing our
own thing in the afternoon. But then life had a way of
playing unexpected tricks.

Around eleven, I answered the doorbell, and Jimmy
Saunders stood there, looking uncomfortable.

"Hi, Val, is Ailene around?"

"She's still upstairs," I told him.

He looked very disappointed. "I was hoping she and I could go for a ride and have a talk today." His blue eyes looked a little washed out, and there were shadows under them as if he hadn't been sleeping well.

"Come on in. I'll go upstairs and see if I can't get her to come down."

He followed me into the front hall and waited while I trotted up the stairs. Ailene was brushing her hair as I entered her room. She was wearing a light blue robe that accentuated her eyes.

"Jimmy's downstairs. He wants to talk with you."

She frowned deeply, her eyes taking on a troubled look. "I can't see him right now. Just tell him to go away."

"Tell him yourself," I said.

"Come on, Val!"

I faced her angrily. "I'm getting fed up with doing you favors. Jimmy's a really nice guy. I don't know why you dumped him. I don't even care. But you owe him an explanation."

"I can't see him. You don't understand."

"For sure, I don't. And I don't like being caught in the middle—especially if you aren't going to tell me why." But maybe I knew why, I thought with a pang of conscience.

Had I set this whole nightmare in motion with my witch wish? It seemed like the new Ailene was turning out to be even worse than the old one.

She dismissed me with a patrician wave of her hand. I was too disgusted with her attitude to stay in the room with her, so I just went back downstairs. But Mother had already discovered Jimmy, and she was talking to him.

"I'm sorry, my daughter tells me she doesn't plan to date you anymore." Mother's manner was cool and controlled. She was dressed in a navy jogging suit, which fit her tall, trim figure perfectly.

Jimmy hung his head despondently and didn't respond.

"Actually, Jimmy's here to see me today," I said, putting my hand through his arm.

Mother's eyebrows shot up in disbelief. I had to admit, it did seem pretty far-fetched, even to me. But I wanted to give him a chance to hang out for a while just in case Ailene changed her mind about seeing him, although I knew that wasn't likely. I led Jimmy to the family room where Dad was sitting, still immersed in the Sunday papers. He looked up and gave Jimmy a smile of recognition.

"Nice to see you again," he said. "Did Ailene have a change of heart?"

"Jimmy and I were just on our way out for a walk," I explained.

I quickly opened the sliding glass doors and dragged Jimmy into the backyard. He was hardly about to refuse. When we walked down our hillside and off into the woodlands, Jimmy turned to me.

"She won't see me, will she?" He stabbed his hand miserably through the shock of sand-colored hair. "I just don't understand it. One day we're happy together, the next she won't even speak to me. We didn't even have an argument or anything. It's got me crazy! Ailene isn't a flighty girl—there has to be an explanation. I can't even concentrate on my ball-playing anymore. I've got to see her."

A perfumed spring breeze embraced us as we walked along. Jimmy thrust his hands into the pockets of his jeans. He looked totally dejected and heart-broken. I could definitely relate.

"I'll do anything I can to help you," I said and meant it.

He smiled at me. "You're a good friend, but I don't know if you can help me."

"When we go back to the house, I'll try again."

"Just tell me, is she seeing Ray Zanka? Did she go out with him last night?"

I hesitated, but I suppose he had a right to know. "Yeah, they were out together yesterday. They went out on his bike."

All the color drained from Jimmy's face. "My God, that's just what I was afraid of! He's not for her. How can I make her see that?" He pulled the collar of his varsity jacket up around his ears defiantly. "There's got to be a way to reach her. If only she'd let me know what's bothering her."

"I'll do what I can," I promised.

We stayed outside for another fifteen minutes and then went back in through the front way. We found Ailene in the kitchen drinking a cup of coffee.

She looked really upset to see that Jimmy was with me. "What are you doing here?" she asked accusingly.

"I came to talk to you."

She turned her back. "Just go. Nothing's changed."

He put his hand on her shoulder, and she tried to shrug it off. "I can't stand not seeing you anymore."

"You'll have to get used to it. Do I have to remind you? Next fall we're at different schools anyway."

"You know that's not what I mean. Come on, Ailene, what's going on with you? Let me in!"

She shook her head, still refusing to look at him. My father came into the kitchen and observed the scene.

"Young man, I think you better leave." His tone was not unkind, but it was firm.

"Yes, sir," Jimmy said reluctantly. "Goodbye, Ailene, for now anyhow." He stalked through to the front hall with me following him. "I'll be in touch," he said. "Thanks." He leaned forward and kissed me on my forehead, a brotherly kiss. Then he was gone.

I hurried back to the kitchen, furious with my sister. "How can you be so cruel to him?"

"Stay out of my face! My life isn't some soap opera you can turn on for your personal amusement and entertainment."

When she turned around, her eyes were filled with tears, and some overflowed onto her pale cheeks. She reminded me of a solitary flower caught in a rainstorm. For a moment, I actually felt sorry for her.

I went back to the rec room where Dad was reading his newspaper, drinking a cup of coffee, and listening to a news program, simultaneously. I paced the room a couple of times, thinking he was unaware of me.

"This would seem like a perfect time for you to study your math," he said, glancing up.

I groaned at him. "We've got tomorrow off. It's Memorial Day. So I can study then."

He set down his cup on an end table. "On the other hand, you might decide you want to go somewhere tomorrow. Since you're not busy now, grab a book. You can study in here."

I did what he asked without further argument. I liked to think of myself as a rebel, but I guess it was just a pose because the desire for approval—not that I ever got much of it—often won out. I returned, book in hand, and got down to studying. About fifteen minutes later, Ailene, now dressed, came quickly into the room.

"Dad, I'm going out. A friend called, and we made up to meet in a little while."

My mother heard this as she walked into the room from the other door. Her usually calm, cool eyes looked anything but tranquil now. "Who exactly is this friend you're meeting?" Mom's gaze was level and frosty as a lake in winter.

"Just a friend. What's the difference? I'm letting you know as a courtesy."

"You are, are you? It couldn't be that Hell's Angel you're planning to meet, is it?"

"I wish you wouldn't refer to Ray in that manner." Ailene's tone was just as icy as Mom's.

It was getting to be like the Arctic Circle in our so-called family room. I felt like wearing a parka.

"Call him back and tell him you aren't going to see him today or any other day."

Ailene was trembling with indignation. "I won't do

that. I am old enough to choose my own friends."

"Not boys like that." Mother slammed her hand down on an end table, a gesture very uncharacteristic of her.

"I happen to like him. And I will find a way to see him even if you don't approve."

We all stared at Ailene in disbelief. It was the first time in her life she ever directly opposed Mother. If they disagreed, Ailene deferred to Mom's judgment, whether it was a significant matter or a trivial one. Ailene had always asked Mom's opinion about everything. I was the one who wouldn't listen and followed my own instincts. This was so unlike Ailene that I doubted my own eyes and ears.

"I cannot allow you to do this," Mother said. She turned to my father. "She has to be punished." The look on Dad's face told me how impossible this situation was for him.

"Mom," I said, turning her attention away for a moment, "Ray is a decent guy. I know you set a lot of store by appearances, but he's not what you think."

"Am I supposed to relent because of that fantastic recommendation? The boy only looks like scum, but underneath he's actually half-way human?" She turned back to Ailene. "Is that what we've brought you up for? We've made sacrifices so that you could grow up living well. Thank goodness you're going away to a fine college in the fall where you'll meet the best sort of young men."

Ailene cast her eyes down. "Mother, that's something I've been meaning to talk to you about. I am not sure I want to go to college, after all. I've been giving it some thought, and I think I need to find myself first."

This was worse than shaking a red cape in front of a charging bull. Mother was beside herself with rage. Her words were barely coherent. She began sputtering.

Dad came and stood beside her. "What exactly would you like to do with yourself?" he asked. His voice sounded like the calm at the center of a hurricane.

"I don't know," Ailene replied with a shrug. "I haven't really thought that part out yet."

"Maybe you could go to work in the supermarket like Val's little friend," Mother said, her words dripping with sarcasm.

"Nothing wrong with that," I said. "At least it's honest labor."

"You stay out of this," Mother warned me.

"Sure, I'll just sit down and study my school work, while everybody else in this house goes crazy."

"As for you, young lady, you can go to your room and stay there!" Mother was shaking her finger in Ailene's face.

"I won't," Ailene said. "I'm going out."

"If you leave this house now, then don't come back," Mother shouted at her.

"Jan!" Dad looked really upset.

Mother pushed away the restraining hand he tried to put around her. "She can't just do whatever she feels like. She has to know there are consequences for bad behavior. We're her parents. That means we deserve her respect. She should listen and obey us."

"But you're wrong about this," Ailene shouted back.

"I thought we taught you certain values."

"Mother, you, of all people, shouldn't talk to me about values!"

"What exactly does that mean?"

Ailene glanced over at Dad and then bit her lower lip. "You're the last one who has the right to lecture on morality. Don't force me to say any more. You'll be very sorry if I do."

"This has gone too far," Dad said, putting himself bodily between Ailene and Mother. "We're all saying hurtful things that we don't mean. Ailene, please don't leave here in anger."

"All right, I'll phone Ray back and tell him I can't go out with him today, but you're being completely unfair."

I let out the breath I hadn't realized I'd been holding.

"There," Dad said with a sigh of relief, "it's going to be fine. Let's compromise. Ailene, you can invite your friend over here instead. I'll sit down and talk to him."

"No, she can't see him at all," Mother said, her voice shrill.

"I'm saying that she can." Dad turned back to Ailene. "However, if he's going to be allowed to date you, it's important he understand a few ground rules. As I said, I'm trying to negotiate a compromise here. Unless you want it your mother's way."

"I'll phone him back," Ailene said quickly.

"All right, have it your way for now," Mother capitulated. But I could tell *now* wasn't going to last for long.

Ray arrived at our house a half-hour later. He was dressed in a T-shirt that sported the garage logo on it and faded jeans that molded tightly to his lean muscular body. Although Mom was very rude to him, Ray was polite to her. Mother wouldn't go near him. She turned up her nose as if she were smelling week-old fish or rotting fruit and walked away.

Dad invited Ray to join Ailene, himself, and me in the family room.

We talked for a while. The atmosphere was tense. Dad spoke directly to Ray after making a little small talk.

"I think you should know that both our daughters have led sheltered lives. We have certain rules for our girls. For one thing, there's a curfew: nine p.m. on school nights and midnight on weekends. We also like to know where our girls are going and with whom. Are you able to respect and comply with our expectations?"

"No problem," Ray said. "I got plenty of respect for you and your daughters."

Finally, Ailene looked as if she couldn't stand it anymore. "Dad, I want to take Ray for a walk, if that's all right."

He indicated that it was, and they quickly took off.

Mother came into the rec room. Her face was like a thunderstorm. "I can't stand the sight of him," she said.

"Why don't you go for a swim at your health club? It'll relax you. I'll take care of things here," Dad said.

"Certainly, the way you took care of the mouse?"

Dad groaned. "Jan, I don't intend to exterminate the boy just for wanting to date my daughter."

"You're too soft," she accused. She ran out of the room, and a few minutes later, the front door slammed.

Dad just stared at the door miserably for a few seconds then buried his nose back in the newspaper.

"She has such a rotten temper," I said.

Dad's hazel eyes met mine. "Your mother means well. But she needs to be on top of a situation."

"She's a total control freak."

"You're not in a position to make judgments. Your mother feels she knows what's best for you girls. This business with Ailene is making her miserable."

Ailene and Ray didn't return to the house for at least an hour. When they did come into the family room, they were holding hands. Ailene was flushed, and her lips looked puffy.

"Daddy, Ray has a terrific idea for Memorial Day. He's going to take me to an amusement park. I haven't been to one in a couple of years."

Ailene knew very well Mom would be furious that she hadn't broken up with Ray. Dad was no pushover, but Ailene was aware, just as I was, that our father was always more agreeable and fair-minded, especially toward women and most especially to the females in his own family. I think, in the days of chivalry, he would have been a knight in shining armor.

"All right," Dad yielded, "but if you go, you're taking Val too."

That upset Ailene. "She's got her own friends."

"She's going along with you." There was no room for negotiation in that voice.

Terrific, just what I wanted, to be a third wheel again. "No way! I have plans with Toni. She's off tomorrow."

Actually, we hadn't made any special plans, but we were going to hang out together for part of the day.

"Bring Toni along. Ailene, you can drive my car so there's plenty of room for everyone."

Ailene looked ready to cry.

"That's a great idea," Ray said. "Sure, Val, invite your friend along too. It'll be fun." He smiled as if the plan were fine with him. Ray was sort of hard to figure out, but like I'd told my parents, I thought he was really okay.

When I called Toni to tell her, she sounded surprised and unsure.

"I thought you'd like the idea," I said, disappointed by her reaction.

"I do, but going there is an all day thing. I can't leave Kathy alone for that long."

"Bring her too. We're taking Dad's car. It's got plenty of room."

"I don't think so, Val. Honestly, it's going to cost too much. I really need that money for other things."

"If you don't go, then I have to be with Ailene and her boyfriend by myself. Do you know how humiliating that would be? Ray is a nice guy, but I'm going to feel really dumb. And Ailene will resent me tagging along. Please come, and let me treat. You'll be making things a lot easier for all of us. I don't want to act like a chaperone or a spy."

"I can't let you pay for me."

"Trust me, you can. It's my dad's treat." I finally talked her into going. I cajoled her and insisted on paying the admission price for Toni and her little sister. I just wouldn't take no for an answer. As expected, my father thought it was a great idea.

ↀↀↀↀ

Ray did the driving since he knew how to get to the amusement park. He was in a very good mood, the only one of us who was. Ailene first glared at me then ignored my existence.

Toni had no new obvious bruises, yet she was again wearing a long-sleeved shirt on a very warm day. I didn't want to spoil it for her by seeming to pry. She and her sister were entirely too quiet. We had a beautiful ride through rolling farmlands with everything turned green and the smell of newness in the air. I tried to concentrate on the scenery.

Once we got inside the park, everyone sort of relaxed. We were all caught up in the atmosphere of fun and make-believe. People dressed as cartoon characters greeted us in front of a large fountain. A band went by, dressed in uniforms. Off to one side, there was a pavilion with a group playing country and western music, and tables shaded by umbrellas.

"What do you want to do first?" Ray asked indulgently.

"Go on the rides," I said. Toni and Kathy agreed, and so we looked around.

The first big ride that we all went on was the Moon Flume. We had to wait in a long line of people. The approach was very slow. It looked a lot like an Aztec temple. We had to climb lots of steps, and we went higher and higher. For a moment, it seemed as if we might well be climbing to the moon. Then we were seated in a kind of boat with water all around us. The descent was like being sucked along into a whirling vortex, but I felt safe, cradled, and enclosed, until the final slide began. It was like being pushed over a waterfall and thrust downward in seismic shock. I was born, baptized, cleansed, and purified all in one incredible swift moment.

I suddenly heard Ailene scream. "I'm soaking wet!" Ms. Perfect was a mess.

Everyone laughed. We were all in need of towels. We went on, sloshing as we walked. I felt like wringing out my sneakers. But the sun was hot, and we dried out quickly.

By the time we got over by Rolling Thunder, Ailene was ready to take the plunge. The old Ailene never would have gone on a ride like that, but today she was living dangerously. Still, she looked like a peeled squash when she came off the ride. Ray was holding her tightly and she wasn't walking too steadily.

"I think I've been on enough exciting rides for one afternoon," she told him.

"Let's go see a show," he agreed.

So we went to see a high diving demonstration down by the lake. Kathy loved the divers dressed as clowns. Having the most fun of anyone, she wanted to come back later and see the dolphins perform. I got the feeling she'd never in her life been to a place like this.

We stopped to have something to eat on the Street of

Dreams. As we sat outside at the Yum-Yum Palace, eating our billowing ice cream cones, we watched the merry-go-round. I couldn't quite make out the song the calliope was grinding out.

"Okay, what next?" Ray asked.

"See the indoor show and cool off in the air-conditioning for a while," Ailene suggested.

I could tell by the look on Kathy's face that she had her eye on the merry-go-round.

"Maybe we ought to split up for a while," I said. "There's a rock concert at the big arena later. We could meet for that."

Ailene looked delighted, and so did Kathy. As for Toni, she'd spent most of the day just staring at Ray, and not saying much. We agreed to meet back in front of the fountain near the bandstand at four o'clock. Then Ray and Ailene headed off to find the indoor show and Toni, Kathy, and I to check out the rides in the children's section.

Kathy was at sort of an in-between age for rides. Only a few of the children's rides were right for her. But there was a petting zoo, and all three of us had fun feeding the animals.

"I'm glad we came," Kathy said. "This is the most fun I've ever had." She twitched her small, freckled nose like a bunny.

Toni appeared happy too, although every now and then an odd look would come over her delicately featured face, and I knew that she had serious worries she couldn't even forget for a little while.

It was a little after four by the time we finally got back to the fountain, but Ailene and Ray weren't there yet, either. I was glad to be there ahead of them because I didn't want to hear Ailene fuss about it later. When they finally showed up, arm-in-arm, Ailene seemed to be in good spirits.

"There's going to be dancing later at the bandstand by the lake. I want to stay for it."

Nobody was really eager to leave this enchanted place, so we went to the dolphin show, which made Kathy happy. She adored the tricks the trainers had the seals and dolphins perform. Afterwards, we took another ride on the log flume and got soaking wet all over again. By now, even Ailene didn't mind.

We stopped and had foot-long hot dogs for supper. Ray insisted on treating all of us, although we tried to talk him out of it.

"No way," he said. "I'm the luckiest guy in this entire park. I've got the four prettiest girls in the place all to myself, practically a harem."

"I should call you a male chauvinist," Ailene told him, punching him playfully in the arm. Ray flashed a grin at her. He had a unique way of making us all feel very special.

The dancing was fun too—up to a point. A disc jockey was playing, and lots of teenagers had congregated. Ray and Ailene danced together. Toni, Kathy, and I listened contentedly for a time. Then some creepy-looking character came over to Toni and asked her to dance. He was all pimply and covered with tattoos. Toni, shy anyway, literally seemed to shrink away. Maybe it was the dark mirror shades he wore or the weird punk hairstyle, but she stammered her refusal. The guy didn't like being turned down, apparently, because he tried to grab her and make her dance with him.

Ray must have been keeping an eye on us. He came over and shoved the smaller guy away with one hard thrust of his big hand.

"Keep out of this, fella." The weirdo seemed to lack the good sense most people would have when Ray got insistent.

Ray didn't budge. "Wanna dance with him?" Ray asked Toni. She shook her head, and he turned to face the weirdo. "Move on, you're not wanted here."

"Listen, you popped-up steroid freak, this is none of your business."

Ray just stood there between him and Toni like a solid, brick wall without saying another word. His fierce expression said it all.

Idiot Boy came at Ray, fists flying. Ray hit him only once, a blow to the mid-section that sprawled him, moaning, on the ground. The DJ was on his feet, now looking over in our direction.

"Time to get going," Ray said. "We don't need any more grief."

Ailene looked upset and stood staring at the kid lying on the ground. Ray took her arm, and we all just naturally followed along. He guided us quickly toward the main gate.

"Thank you," Toni said, looking at Ray with adoring eyes.

"Hey, I'd do as much for my own sisters," he said.

On the trip home, everyone was quiet, pretty much silent. I guess we were all exhausted. Kathy even fell asleep, drifting off for a time.

Ray drove, and Ailene fooled around with the radio. Once I saw Ailene turn her head as she looked out the window. Then I noticed a tear trickle down her cheek. I wondered what that was all about. The sense of wrongness I intuitively felt as I studied Ailene made me uneasy. I couldn't understand the complex puzzle, the mystery, my sister had become. I so hoped I wasn't to blame.

Chapter 10

Tuesday morning, Ailene could barely move. I doubt she'd ever walked so much in her life. Cheerleading was a different kind of exercise. Since I was used to walking and jogging long distances, my legs were fine, but even I was a tad tired.

There wasn't much table talk at breakfast. Mom was giving everyone the cold shoulder, still angry that Ailene had gone out with Ray, even well-chaperoned. She just sat there, looking drop-dead gorgeous in her tailored gray business suit.

Dad had asked about our day when we arrived home the previous evening and was satisfied that everything was okay.

We skipped over Ray decking the weird kid.

For the first time in quite a while, Ailene offered me a ride to school, and I accepted happily. For one thing, it meant I could leave a little later, and that was appreciated.

We didn't talk much on the drive, but then Ailene had never talked much to me about anything.

That was our family history, sounds of silence. As she pulled her Corvette into the student parking lot, she glanced in the mirror. "I look awful today," she exclaimed, "like a cooked lobster. Just look at my nose! I'll be confused for Rudolf the Red-nosed Reindeer."

"Not at this time of year."

It was true that she had burned more than me, but then she was a lot fairer. She fussed around with make-up before we went into school.

"How's that?"

"Better," I told her.

She seemed relieved. "Next time I'll remember to wear sun block." Mother would have reminded her if they'd been on speaking terms.

It was nice walking along the corridor with Ailene. A lot of boys threw admiring glances in her direction. We parted wordlessly, each going in the direction of our own locker. But at least I knew I had a ride home if I wanted it.

School seemed particularly boring after being off for three days. Senor Varga, our Spanish teacher, showed part of the movie *Stand and Deliver* in Spanish first period, and I nearly dozed off. With ten minutes left in the period, the Senor stopped the movie and told us to write a brief description in Spanish of what we'd watched. Luckily, I'd seen the movie before!

I met Toni for lunch in the cafeteria. Just as we were getting ready to feast on peanut butter and jelly sandwiches, Jimmy came by our table.

"Can I join you for a little while?" he asked. Then he spent the entire period at our table, except for the time on the hot lunch line. Jimmy did most of the talking, telling us about how depressed he felt and how much he wanted Ailene back. At least his unhappiness didn't seem to affect his appetite. He ate more than twice what we did.

"Like I said, Jimmy, I'll do what I can to help. Ailene and I have opened a brand-new channel of communication." I didn't have the heart to tell him all we'd actually discussed was whether or not Ailene resembled a lobster, but that was a start, I reasoned.

"Thanks, Val, you really are a friend." There was genuine gratitude in his voice.

I pictured myself in the guise of Mother Theresa, benevolently doing good deeds for the needy. Was I now going to be a goody-goody? The worse the sinner, the nobler the saint? If I'd lived in another century, I could have been martyred and maybe become a real saint. Then my parents in their old age might have said, "Yes, that angel was our daughter: We're so proud of her."

Maybe they would even have regretted not loving me more. Maybe my mother would have been sorry she only paid attention to Ailene.

I shook away the ridiculous thought and laughed silently at myself. If I were going to be decent and considerate of other people, it would have to be because it made me feel good about myself, because I knew in my own heart it was the right thing to do. Waiting for a pat on the head from Mother—or anyone else, for that matter—wasn't going to work.

I had to get beyond that. It was only when I no longer needed things that I got them anyway.

I remembered how it was when I was small. Mostly, my mother treated me with indifference. So then I'd go and do something she didn't like. In those days, I preferred being yelled at to being ignored. Little kids can act pretty dumb.

I was trying to change for the better now, but Mother couldn't—or didn't want to—see it.

As the bell rang, I asked Toni if she could come over that day.

"I have to work this afternoon," she said. "The first day I'll be free again is next Sunday. Maybe we can get together again late Saturday."

I quickly agreed and told her that she could bring Kathy along if she liked. Toni seemed grateful for the suggestion.

"We had a good time yesterday," she told me. "I don't remember doing anything like that since before my mother left, and, for Kathy, it was really a big deal."

"I'm glad," I said.

"Your sister is so lucky to have a great guy like Ray interested in her," Toni said dreamily.

"Yeah, she's got a gift for collecting terrific guys, just like some people collect rocks or baseball cards."

ᆭᄋᆭ

Ailene did give me a ride home after school, but we didn't go directly back to the house.

"I have to stop for gas," she told me.

Of course, she drove out of her way to stop at Ray's station. While the man was filling up the tank, Ailene got out and went back to the garage. A few minutes later, Ray emerged with her, and they walked back to the car where I was sitting and waiting.

"This little visit brightens my day," he said with a big grin. He kissed Ailene on the lips without touching her, his hands behind his back. "You're too beautiful to get dirty and grimy like I am, but you're also irresistible."

She did look vibrantly alive. Sunlight danced in her golden hair. She leaned toward him, and they kissed again. He let out a deep sigh. "How am I going to concentrate on a brake job after this?"

"Call me tonight," Ailene said. Her voice was sultry and seductive. For sure Ray would be phoning her.

His grease-stained shirt was soaked through with perspiration, and he removed it, throwing it over his shoulder as Ailene paid for the gas and started the engine again. He looked powerful enough to lift up any car on the lot on those broad shoulders, a regular Atlas. I let out a deep sigh.

A girl would have to be dead not to find Ray Zanka attractive.

When we got home, our phone was ringing. It was Dave.

"Can I come over today?"

I told him he was welcome, and he seemed delighted. I didn't tell Ailene about his call though. She was upstairs in her room when Dave arrived. Of course, he asked for her immediately.

"Ailene's resting right now. She's tired. We had a busy day yesterday."

He looked disappointed, his brown eyes darkening. "Did you have a nice holiday?" he asked politely.

"It was okay," I replied. I wasn't going to tell him about our amusement park outing, just like I hadn't mentioned it to Jimmy. It would have made them feel worse. "How was your Memorial Day?"

He shrugged, removing his glasses and following me into the rec room. "Kind of dull. Dad barbecued out in the yard, and my parents invited some of the neighbors over. Been studying your geometry?"

"Trying, anyway. I think the exam is going to be treacherous. I've got to do well on it. If I can at least get a C, then I'll pull it for the year."

"Assuming you get a C for the marking period."

"Right, but since you started tutoring me, I'm doing much better on the Friday quizzes. I really do understand how to analyze the problems now."

"Good. It's just a matter of hard work and self-discipline," he said.

"Is that all?"

He smiled and brushed back the lock of hair that always fell across his forehead. "You've got the grit. If you can run long distance, you can pass geometry."

"What's one thing got to do with the other?"

"Simple, they both demand dedication and determination. If you've got the stamina for one, then you've got it for the other. Haven't you noticed that a lot of hard-working, intelligent students go out for long distance running?"

"I never thought about it," I told him. "Now that you mention it, this applies to you too."

He looked at me out of the corner of one eye. "How do you mean?"

It was my turn to smile at him. "Well, it seems to me that you're a real brain and a hard worker as well. There-fore, you should be willing to start a program of physical exercise which will have long term health benefits."

"You sound just like my Phys Ed teacher. Ugh!"

I ignored his remark. "After you finish helping me with my schoolwork, we can go jogging."

He protested loudly. "It's too hot out there!"

"Not by the time we'll be going to the track."

"I have to do my own homework."

"You can do that when you get home tonight."

"I forgot to bring my sneakers." He smiled in triumph.

"You don't live so far from here. I'll come along with you while you change. If you like, you can have dinner at our house with the family—and Ailene. I'll tell my par-ents I invited you."

That was the selling point. He finally gave in, and I considered a future in used car sales.

We had just settled into our work when the phone rang. In case Ailene was asleep, I picked up the extension in the family room. The voice on the other end was an adult asking to speak to either Mr. or Mrs. Williams. I explained that they were both still at work. The disembodied male voice sounded annoyed.

"You can leave a message," I offered.

It turned out to be Mr. Hartman, the Assistant Principal of Wilson High. I started to sweat. At our school, Mr. Hartman is referred to as "the enforcer." What could I have done to warrant a call from Heartless Hartman to my parents? Although I was far from the best student at school, I really wasn't a troublemaker anymore, unless you called a few wisecracks severely punishable.

"I'll give my parents the message that you called," I assured him.

"Do that," he said in a voice that sent chills slithering down my spine.

"Can I tell them what you are calling in reference to?" I wondered if he'd have me hung for splitting an infinitive. My grammar always was bad news.

"I prefer to discuss the matter with them."

"But they'll want more information."

There was a hesitation at the other end. "To whom am I speaking?"

"This is Val Williams. Is there something I should know?"

"This call is in reference to Ailene. You will give the message to your parents?"

I assured him I would. After he hung up, I sat there staring off into space and wondering in astonishment what Ailene could ever have done to draw the attention of our school executioner.

"Val? Something wrong?" Dave drew my attention back to the present moment.

"No," I said evasively, "just taking a message for my folks." I decided not to bother Ailene with the information. She'd find out soon enough. But what could she have done?

Dave and I worked through the set of geometry problems I'd been given for homework. Then I went upstairs and changed into jogging shorts and a lightweight T-shirt. I checked on Ailene and found she was asleep, so I didn't disturb her. Arriving downstairs where Dave was waiting, I insisted that we go back to his house so he could change.

By the time we got to his development, the day had turned cloudy.

"Looks like rain," he said. "Guess we can't go jogging after all."

"Only a wimp would let a little cloud cover scare him off," I challenged.

The housing development where Dave lived was older than ours and not as fancy, but the houses were more individualized. The streets were tree-lined and there with children out playing, which gave the area a friendly look. Dave's house was a cheery yellow-shingled ranch with a double garage.

I followed him inside a little hesitantly. He called out and was greeted by a large golden Lab who jumped on him enthusiastically. I stepped back.

Dave noticed my discomfort. "He won't bite. He's just a big, friendly fellow."

"If you say so. When I see a dog that size, I think he sees 'hamburger' written across my forehead."

Dave smiled, clearly pleased to have the upper hand. "I won't sic him on you, no matter how much you irritate me. Truman really is a good dog, aren't you, boy?" As if to underscore this, the dog gave a slobbering lick to my hand. "See, he likes you. He wants to kiss you."

"I'm glad somebody wants to, even if it is just a dog."

"Truman isn't just any dog. Mom named him after Harry Truman because he's got character just like the former president. He even looks like ol' Harry."

That was a bit of a stretch, but the dog did grow on you. The tail kept on wagging, and the long, pink tongue panted in welcome.

"Didn't you ever have a pet?"

"No, Mom doesn't like them. Ailene once asked for a kitten, and Mom said no because animals are a nuisance, a bother she didn't have time for. Anyway, she said we might be allergic."

"That's too bad. Truman's been better than most kids to be around. Never a nasty word from him. No bullying. I think my parents got him for me because I'm an only child. They were afraid I'd be lonely."

Dave's mother gave the immediate impression of being a very nice lady. She offered us milk and chocolate chip cookies, which Dave was quite willing to take. But I explained that we couldn't eat until after we ran. His mother and I sat and talked while Dave went to his bedroom to change.

"I'm so glad you're spending time with Dave," his

mother said. She had a friendly smile and wore thick glasses just like her son.

"Dave's a good guy," I told her.

"Yes, he is. But he doesn't seem to make friends very easily. I suppose it's because he spends most of his time studying. He's not as developed socially as he is intellectually."

When Dave returned, I noticed he didn't look half bad in shorts, although his muscles definitely needed toning. I checked my watch: it was five-thirty.

"Let's head over to the school track. I think the teams are about done with their practices. We can have the place practically to ourselves now."

There was a nice breeze at the track and the place was nearly deserted as I had predicted.

"Okay, what do we do first?" Dave asked.

"We walk around the track twice to loosen up, and then we stretch our muscles. That way we won't be stiff and sore tomorrow. It also helps prevent injuries."

I enjoyed being the teacher for once. We talked about different things as we walked. Dave told me a little more about himself and his dreams. As I listened to him talk about his love for science, it occurred to me that I didn't have goals the way he did. I wondered if I ever would.

I showed him how to use the chain link fence that surrounded the track as a support for stretching exercises. He looked pretty silly at one point stretching his legs out as far as they would go, but I didn't laugh because I knew that he was sincerely trying. Then we took off, just moving easily. He held with me for one full mile, but then waved me on.

"You need to cool down slowly," I called back to him. "Do what we did before. Walk around the track twice for a half-mile and then stretch. I just want to put in some extra time." I took off then, picking up my pace considerably. Since I wasn't going out for distance this time, I wanted to get a nice workout. I paced myself for another quarter, and then I raced at top speed. Overhead the sun came out, and I felt spring blossoming into summer. I wasn't some old turtle anymore.

I was a meteor flashing through time and space. I felt so alive, as if I was immortal!

As I approached the final hundred yards, I kicked out until there was no breath left in me, and I was ready to collapse. I won my race against myself. I slowed down gradually until I was walking again.

Dave came up alongside me. He put his arm around me. I felt my shoulders tingle at his touch. "You okay?" he asked. "Wow, you were impressive."

I smiled, hoping that when I got back to competition again, I would be outstanding. Even if I didn't know yet what I wanted to study, I knew that winning a track scholarship to college was important to me.

When we finished, it was well after six. Dave drove us back to my house. My mother had already come home. I could hear her out in the kitchen.

Dave and I went to say hello.

"Either you or Ailene should have started dinner," Mother said crossly.

"Ailene's been asleep, and Dave and I went out to the track. I've got to take a shower right away," I told her. "Otherwise, it won't be pleasant to have me around. But I'll help when I come down. By the way, I invited Dave to stay. I hope that's all right."

Suddenly, Mom was all smiles. "Of course, it's okay! Ailene will be delighted." She turned to me again. "Your father will help me fix something. It's such a hot day I think a salad will do. Make sure Ailene is awake when you go upstairs and send her down here to greet our guest."

I could hear Mother chirping away at Dave as I ran upstairs. I went to tell Ailene about what Mother had said. Ailene was awake, just lying in the dark, staring listlessly at the ceiling, a moody expression on her face, nothing like the energetic girl she used to be.

"Better get downstairs. The Queen Mum is requesting an audience with you." I thought she looked annoyed with me. "No need to thank me." Then I hurried off to the bathroom.

෴

By the time I was washed and changed, Dad had arrived home, and I was glad to see him.

Dinner was, as Mom had said, very light. In fact, it was so light that I was still hungry after we finished eating, but I kept my mouth shut, for once.

"I'm so glad that you came over today, Dave," my mother said. "You're good company for Ailene. Val, could you help with the dishes? Ailene, you can take

Dave into the living room. You might want to talk about your plans for college next year. Dave, you are going to Boston too, aren't you?" Mother presented her most charming smile.

Dave took Ailene's arm. My sister looked less than pleased. They were headed toward the living room when the telephone rang.

"I'll get it," Ailene said, quickly grabbing the kitchen phone before Mom could get it.

What amazing reflexes Ailene had when it suited her. She listened to the voice at the other end, and a big smile appeared on her face. "It's for me. I'll just take that in my room. Val, hang up when I tell you to."

Mother looked upset.

Dad took over at that point. "Dave, why don't you join me? We'll let the women do the dirty work out here and relax for a while."

So Dave and my father watched the news in the family room, and I helped Mom clean up. Now and then, I caught snatches of their conversation because Mom didn't bother talking to me at all. It amazed me: my father was actually telling Dave about me, not Ailene. And everything he said was complimentary. I wanted to go in there and hug him. Instead, I sponged down the kitchen table.

When Ailene returned, she was cheerful. I could only think that Ray had phoned her. These days, he seemed to be the one person that made her feel happy. Otherwise, she was constantly looking depressed.

"I'm going out for a while," she said.

Mother bit down on her lower lip. "Where are you going?" Her eyes darkened like a storm at sea.

"I have a right to go for a drive, don't I?"

"Not alone. It's almost dark. I'll ask Dave to go with you."

Ailene raised her hand in a halting gesture. "No, Mother, you won't. I like Dave as a friend, but don't try to push him on me." Then she took off through the kitchen door before Mom could say another word.

"I want to talk to you later," Mother called after her.

When Dave heard that Ailene had left, he decided it was time for him to go home too. After he'd gone, Mom turned to Dad and me.

"He'd be perfect for her. I don't know why she doesn't see it. Where's her common sense? Did you see how he looks at her? He idolizes her. And that boy is destined to be successful."

I walked away and went upstairs to my room. Sure, I saw the way Dave looked at Ailene, but I tried not to think about it. I felt like crying when Mother brought it up. Why had I bothered to insist that Dave go jogging with me? He'd never look at me the way he did at Ailene. I just wasn't pretty enough, smart enough, or nice enough. I lay down on my bed suddenly feeling miserable and exhausted.

ℰↃℰↃ

It was the next morning before I remembered to tell my parents about Mr. Hartman's phone call. I had meant to warn Ailene first, but the occasion didn't present itself. I fell asleep before Ailene returned.

Dad fixed breakfast for us as he often did. Between the Cheerios and the muffins, I cleared my throat and told my parents about the phone call. Ailene was just entering the kitchen.

Mother turned to confront her immediately. "What did you do to get into trouble?"

Ailene turned on me. "I suppose you just had to tell them?"

I stood up. "He'd only go on calling back until he gets hold of them. You know he's a regular bulldog."

"I might have expected problems with Val, but in four years of high school, this is the first time we've ever had problems with you, Ailene."

"It's no big deal. I just decided to cut out one day last week. My English teacher picked up on it."

Mother gave her a stony stare. "You cut school? How dare you?"

"That's exactly it, Mother, I never have dared. Everyone does, but not me. A lot of seniors cut. I've always been such a good little girl and done everything you told me to do. I never questioned you. Never once did I think for myself."

"If getting into trouble at school is your idea of thinking for yourself, then I should arrange a lobotomy for you."

"I believe you already have." With that, Ailene ran out of the kitchen. We heard her driving off a minute or two later.

"What is going on in that girl's head?"

"I'll phone Mr. Hartman from the office later," Dad said solemnly.

"No, you won't. I want to talk with him myself. I need to hear the whole story."

My stomach suddenly felt sick. I hated being involved in this constant bickering. Worse still was the thought that I was probably to blame for everything that had gone wrong with my family.

Dinnertime in our kitchen was another battle in a continuing family war.

"Mr. Hartman tells me not only did you cut that day last week, but several of your teachers are concerned about you. You've always been an exemplary student, and now suddenly you're failing tests and not handing in homework. What is going on? I want to know."

"Maybe it's just a case of senioritis," Dad suggested. "You know how they slump off at the end of school once the college acceptances are in."

"Not our Ailene. She's always been conscientious about everything."

"Mother, I don't want to be *your* Ailene anymore. You act like you know everything. Well, you're wrong about a lot of things. It took me a long time to realize that. I was totally naïve." With that, she got up and left the table.

"What's wrong with her? What's happened to our wonderful girl?" Mother said, dissolving into tears.

Father went and put his arms around her.

I left them alone together and decided it was time Ailene, and I had a real talk. Even if I couldn't take back

my wish, I was determined to do something to make matters right.

Chapter 11

Ailene hadn't bothered to turn on her lamp. The shades were down, and the room was nearly dark. She was pacing back and forth, her hands folded in front of her. "I suppose Mom or Dad sent you up here?" She eyed me with mistrust.

"No, there are a lot of people concerned about you, and I just happen to be one of them."

"I don't know what everyone is so worried about."

"It probably has something to do with a complete personality change overnight. You haven't been acting yourself."

She turned and faced me directly. "And just who am I, exactly?"

"My sister and I happen to care about you."

"Since when?" Her eyes were hard blue steel cutting into me like knife blades.

"Hey, that's not fair!"

"Yes, it is. You've always hated me. So why all of a sudden would you care?"

"Maybe because you've stopped acting like Princess Perfect."

"So you admit that's what you thought of me?"

"It's how you act." I had gone into her room to offer comfort and counsel, but I had the uncomfortable feeling I was being held by the Inquisition and would soon be tortured on the rack. "I admit I was jealous because you're so beautiful and popular. Mom and Dad love you more. In fact, everybody loves you."

"Not my sister," she retorted, a caustic edge to her voice.

"I just wished you would act human sometimes."

"And now that I am, you're concerned about me?" She gave me a mistrustful glance out of the corner of her eye.

"You've been behaving a little too human."

Should I have told her about my wish, how maybe it had been responsible for the change in her personality? But was that even true—and even if it was, would my sister believe such a thing was possible? She'd be scornful.

Ailene laughed, a hollow sound. "What if I said that I looked in the mirror one morning not too long ago and wondered who and what I was? I've always done exactly what I was told to do. I knew what society expected of me. I've been a total conformist. I never dared to be different. I never had a single thought or idea of my own."

"I understand."

She pointed an accusing finger at me. "Don't you say

that, because you do not understand. You've always done whatever you wanted."

I just sat there staring at her angry face. "I wasn't given any other choice. Nobody was paving the way for me."

"At least you know who you are, and what you want. I don't. I spent my entire life trying to please other people and live up to their expectations. If something hadn't happened to jolt me, I would have spent the rest of my life living exactly that way. I've gone through high school like a zombie, not even truly alive. I'm practically brain dead."

I shook my head in denial. "Ailene, you're so popular. You've been involved in every important school activity and function. All the guys are crazy about you, and all the girls want to be your friend. How can you say you haven't lived?"

"I'm always so busy, so rushed, balancing a million activities, and studying like a maniac. I'm tired of it all. I've had it. I'm taking time out. Did you know Jimmy wanted to get serious? He started talking about how we'd get engaged in maybe a year or so. I could see my whole life planned out ahead of me. Just doing the right and proper thing because it's expected. Do you have any idea how much that frightens me?"

"I think you ought to have told Jimmy how you felt instead of just dumping him like that. He deserved better."

She looked as if she were ready to cry. "Jimmy is a terrific guy."

"Why don't you phone him? He's really hurting."

Her eyes shined too brightly. "And tell him what? That I'm confused about a lot of things right now, that I don't know my own mind?"

"It would be better than letting him think you don't care about him anymore."

"I never told him that." A large teardrop welled over her eye and dripped down her cheek.

"Maybe if you talked to Mom or Dad about this—"

"No, absolutely not! I can't discuss important things with either of them."

"They love you."

She began pacing the room again like a caged tigress. "They love their 'Perfect Princess,' as you refer to me. I haven't been that lately, have I? Mom loves me on her terms. I have to live up to her expectations. She only wants to hear the good things. I can't tell her the bad ones. I can't tell her how I feel because she doesn't want to hear about it. She won't help me."

"Maybe she can't," I said, realizing something for the first time. "I mean, maybe she's not as sure of herself as we always thought."

Ailene stopped pacing and looked at me questioningly. "Is that possible?" She seemed surprised.

"Sure, why not? You know how angry Mom gets when anything out of the ordinary happens, or we don't behave the way she expects? Maybe it's because she's frightened."

"There are things she's done, things that can't be for-given." Ailene looked troubled.

I felt confused. Her cryptic comment made no sense. "What are you talking about?"

Ailene shook her head. "It's better you don't know."

I was puzzled by her attitude. Why wouldn't Ailene tell me why she was suddenly so down on our mother? But I'd never been in her confidence, so why should she trust me now?

"I still half expect you to slop bubble gum in my hair when my back is turned." She was looking at me speculatively.

"Ailene, I haven't done anything like that since I was ten! I'm really trying to be a better person. I guess I used to think the only way people would notice me was if I acted out. The only time Mom noticed me was to holler at me for doing something wrong. I realize now that all I accomplished was making me feel rotten about myself."

"So no more listening in on my private conversations?"

Ailene again viewed me out of the corner of her eye, arms still folded.

"Hey, I'm changing, but it takes time. No one's perfect. Can you be satisfied with good intentions?"

Ailene seemed calmer now. She even smiled at me. Then she went to her dresser and opened her jewelry box. Ailene removed something and came toward me, thrusting a shiny, gold heart into my hand. "I want you to have this," she told me.

I looked down at the fine necklace and the puffy heart attached to it. "I can't take it! This is the gold heart Mom gave you for your birthday last year."

She put her hand over mine as I tried to return it to her. "No, you must take it. I've shared my heart with you today for the first time ever. This will be a symbol of that."

I put my arms around Ailene and hugged her tightly. "I want to help you," I told her.

"Okay, great...then tell me how you think I'd look with a tattoo."

I must have just gawked at her open-mouthed because she laughed.

"You were only kidding, right?"

"Not really. I was thinking I might like one on my ankle. Maybe a small, tasteful red heart."

"You really want to drive Mom and Dad crazy? She'll freak out, and he'll have a heart attack."

"If I intended that, I'd do something more dramatic, maybe get some piercing done, you know, like in my navel."

"Why stop there? Why not wear a nose ring or one through your tongue?"

"Interesting idea, sis."

"There's some really weird-looking people in our school. I guess they think they're making a statement of individuality. The artsy crowd does a lot of the piercing stuff. Karen Lawrence has rainbow-colored hair: green, blue, orange, and purple. Some people think that's really cool. Then there's Dana Witherspoon who claims she's a vampire, wears long black skirts, black lipstick, and nail polish and even dyed her hair black. Can you see yourself with the goth look? Want me to continue enumerating possibilities?"

"Okay, I get your point. Maybe I don't need to be totally radical." Ailene smiled, but just for a moment.

I went to my room, placed Ailene's jewelry gift on top of my dresser, and then rooted around in the bottom of my closet. I found the music box and opened it.

"I want to take back my wish. Please!"

Nothing happened. In despair, I shut the box and shoved it back into the closet. *There is no such thing as magic*, I told myself. But I couldn't shake the feeling there were forces at work that couldn't be controlled, and I was the one who'd set them in motion. I swallowed hard.

৩৩৩

The following morning, after the folks left for work, Ailene said she wasn't feeling well enough to go to school.

"You're not cutting again!"

"I'm really not feeling well. I'm going to stay in bed."

I hoped our talk might have helped Ailene, but she still seemed depressed, and I didn't know what to do about it. It was hard for me to concentrate on schoolwork that morning. The problem was compounded at lunchtime when I saw Toni. There was a nasty discoloration on her cheek, and she was moving as if she ached all over.

"Are you all right?"

"Why shouldn't I be?" The scared look was back.

"You're bruised again."

Her eyes wouldn't meet mine. Her mouth was a twisted ribbon. "I banged into something at work."

"Let me see. I'm good at fixing up pains. I often get injured when I run in races."

She put her hand over her face. "No, it's nothing really."

When I put my hand on her arm, she cringed as if in agony. I took a deep breath, about to do something I had never done before in the history of our friendship.

"Roll up your sleeve for just a minute," I insisted.

Finally, she complied with my request. I couldn't believe what I was looking at. Her entire arm was black and blue, and a large red welt had swelled up near the elbow. She quickly rolled the sleeve down again, looking around as if to make certain no one else had seen it. She looked like a hunted animal.

"Ice," I said, recovering myself. "You need to put ice on and off for a few minutes every couple of hours."

"Thanks, Doctor."

"I got that advice from the trainer when I hurt my knee."

We continued eating our sandwiches, except neither one of us could really eat. Toni was withdrawn and silent. Finally, I couldn't stand it anymore.

"I don't suppose you'd like to tell me how you really got those bruises?"

"Let's just say I'm accident prone."

"You don't need to lie to me. It isn't right."

"I don't want to talk about it, Val. Please, no more questions. If you're really my friend, you won't interrogate me. Okay?"

We didn't speak to each other again. What was there to say? Despite nearly two years of friendship, Toni obviously didn't trust me enough to be honest. Could I have really helped her anyway? Probably not, I rationalized. I tried my best to forget about her problems. But I found I couldn't.

There was a substitute in health ed, the last period of the day. She handed us a photocopy with a busywork assignment on it. No one was exactly working too hard on it. One girl put up her book so she could lean a mirror against it and apply eye make-up while two others were passing notes. One boy shuffled his feet against the floor.

I was feeling agitated. Finally, I made a decision. I raised my hand and asked if I could leave the room. At first, the sub refused. I guess she figured I was just trying to get out so I could roam the halls. But I explained I had to see my guidance counselor and that it was urgent. I finally bugged her enough, I guess, because she ended up letting me go.

It did feel great being out in the hall, like a prisoner who'd been freed from a cell, but too soon I was standing in front of the guidance office. I opened the door nervously. The secretary looked up from her typing, and I explained I needed to see any counselor that was free. Normally at Wilson, we had to fill out a request form, except when it was some kind of an emergency, and then they did let you come in.

Mr. Burns, the head counselor, was in his office, only I had to wait a few minutes to see him. I sat in the outer office, wondering if I was doing the right thing. I ripped anxiously at my fingernails. Would Toni hate me after this? Maybe I would only talk about a hypothetical friend.

Mr. Burns at first seemed annoyed to be bothered. Then I explained to him that I was concerned about a possible child abuse case, and he became attentive.

"What seems to be the problem?"

"Well, my friend always has bruises on her. Sometimes, they're really bad ones, like today."

"Have you asked her about them?" His eyes seemed to be measuring me.

"Yes, but she just says she's accident-prone."

"But you don't think so?"

"She's good in gym. She never falls or anything. And her father doesn't seem like a very nice person. I think she's afraid of him."

Mr. Burns scratched his chin thoughtfully. "This is a very serious accusation."

"I know," I agreed miserably.

"Can you get this girl to see me?"

"I don't think so."

"Why don't you give me her name, and I'll have her guidance counselor call her in."

I hesitated, worrying my lower lip. This was exactly what I was afraid of. "Maybe I ought to talk to her again before I do that."

Mr. Burns nodded his head. "That might be wise. However, please don't wait too long. If it is a case of child abuse, matters usually get worse rather than better. You have an obligation to your friend to do the right thing, even if she gets mad at you."

After promising that I would come back again in a few days, I left the guidance office feeling troubled. I was bothered about Toni and also concerned about Ailene. Maybe it was true:

I had no life of my own, so I was busy snooping around in those of other people. But was it wrong to get involved when you saw people suffering? Then a weird thought stopped me dead in my tracks—I had always liked Toni but I'd actually begun to care about Ailene! Maybe I didn't hate her anymore.

I think I read somewhere there was a fine line between love and hate.

Out in the hall, someone called my name. I turned, and there was Mr. Schmidt. "Nice job on that last article, Williams. You show potential. Might make a real journalist out of you one of these days."

He actually smiled at me.

Funny how those few words of praise made me feel good inside.

෴

It was raining pretty hard when I got out to the bus. It looked like an all day drencher. I didn't feel much like running in the rain and was glad that I wasn't on spring track, so I didn't have to.

On the bus, I opened my English book to the homework. All we had to read were some poems.

The first one was titled "Richard Cory" by some writer named Edwin Arlington Robinson. The name seemed kind of pretentious, but I liked the poem right off because it was really short.

Richard Cory, it seemed, was this guy who was rich as a king and imperially slim. All the "people on the pavement," the ordinary folks, thought he was better than them, and they admired him. Then one day, Richard Cory put a bullet through his head.

The poem shocked me. I had to read it again. I made a scary connection. Richard Cory was just like Ailene, a regal, superior person that everyone admired. No one realized that such an aristocratic individual could have problems just like any ordinary human being. And then Richard Cory killed himself! My God, could Ailene do something like that? Would she?

I thought about her giving me her gold heart. She loved that necklace and wore it all the time. Hadn't we learned in health class that people contemplating suicide often gave away their most prized possessions? I started to sweat, really sweat, not perspire. I was so scared. What might I have done making that horrible, foolish wish?

The bus seemed to be taking forever. It was so slow! Why couldn't it move along a little faster? When I finally got off, I sprinted all the way from the bus stop to my house. I was totally breathless by the time I reached home. I opened the door with my key because it was locked. My hand actually trembled. I listened for a moment but didn't hear a sound.

"Ailene!" I called out in a hoarse, dry voice.

There wasn't any answer. I went running up the stairs calling her name. Still no answer. Finally, I opened the door of her room, my heart pounding unbearably in my chest. She was lying quiet and still on her bed. I ran over and shook her.

"What are you doing?" Her voice was drugged with sleep.

I finally dared to breathe again. "Sorry, I got scared when you didn't answer. I thought something was wrong with you."

She sat up, touching her head. "There is something wrong. I'm running a temperature. Nothing serious though. I'll be fine. It's nice to know you care about me." She smiled warmly.

"I'll go get you a glass of juice."

"That would be great," she said. Then she flopped down on the pillow again and closed her eyes.

"I'll bring you some aspirin too."

Walking down the stairs, I felt pretty lame. Maybe I did have an idiotic imagination. What about Toni? Couldn't I be wrong about her as well? How could I just come out and tell her what I was thinking? It might ruin our friendship.

☙❧☙

In the end, I didn't talk to Toni about her bruises again. But I did invite her over for Saturday, and she accepted. As for things at our house, they were still very strained. Mom and Dad had been invited to have dinner with friends.

Ailene didn't mention Saturday at all, but Ray did call

several times, and I knew she had plans, even if my parents didn't know about it.

On Friday evening, I was reflecting on what I might be doing on the weekend when the telephone rang. It was Toni. I thought she was calling to tell me whether or not she was bringing Kathy along on Saturday.

"Val, please, I need your help," Toni said, sounding panicky.

Chapter 12

I could tell by the sound of Toni's voice that she was really upset. I could also hear someone crying loudly in the background.

"What's wrong?" I asked.

"It's Kathy. I think her arm might be broken."

"Where's your dad?"

She was silent for a moment. "He's out."

"Will he be back soon?"

"I don't think so." Her terse response told me a lot.

I tried to think. "Can you call emergency? Ask for an ambulance. They'll take you to the closest hospital."

"No hospital! I just need to get her to a doctor." She wasn't making much sense from my point of view, but I assumed she had her reasons.

"Hold on," I said. "I'll ask my dad if he can drive me over. Maybe we can help, or he'll phone our doctor."

She thanked me, and I went to find my father. He was

companionably sharing a cup of coffee with Mom in the kitchen. I told them what had happened.

My mother immediately tensed. "That's what comes of having low-class friends. No parents around to supervise the children. I've always thought your friend Toni seemed like a neglected child."

"Please, Mom, don't start now. She needs our help. That's all that matters."

My father began hunting around for his car keys. Mom, of course, knew exactly where they were and handed them to him.

"You're a soft touch," Mom told him, but not as harshly as I might have expected.

In the car, I thanked my father. "I wish Mom was as understanding as you are."

"She is," he said.

"No, she doesn't have any compassion for other people."

"Actually, she's very sensitive," he said, "maybe too sensitive. Someday, you'll understand."

The front light shone like a beacon on the porch of Toni's small, dilapidated house. Dad only had to knock once. They were waiting for us. Tears streamed down Kathy's small, pale face. Toni seemed relieved to see us.

Dad looked at Kathy's arm and then very carefully touched it in the gentlest manner. "It's broken all right. I can feel the bone pressing through. I'll call Dr. Larsen."

As it turned out, our doctor was not available. He was on vacation, and someone else was on call covering for him. The service suggested that Dad phone for an ambulance. A doctor would meet us at the hospital.

Dad looked over at the faces of the two scared girls. "An ambulance isn't necessary." He hung up the phone and turned to Toni. "I'll be driving you," he said.

At the hospital, they wanted to know right away what kind of insurance coverage Toni's father had. She told them he didn't have any. The woman in charge looked upset, even after Toni said she would pay in installments. My dad stepped in and said that he would take care of the bill.

"I'll take responsibility for whatever the child's care costs," he said.

I was very proud of my father at that moment.

They admitted Kathy through Emergency. We had to wait nearly an hour and a half, but a doctor finally did see Kathy. Another hour passed before her arm was set, and then the doctor began asking questions. Neither Toni nor Kathy seemed to want to answer them.

"It was just an accident," Toni said and bit down on her lower lip, eyes fixed on the floor.

"There seem to be a lot of bruises," the young doctor said suspiciously.

"She fell," Toni said a little too quickly.

My dad exchanged looks with me. The doctor insisted on filling out a detailed report. Afterward, he took my dad aside, and they talked very quietly, but I could tell that it was a very serious discussion.

When Dad returned, he said that Kathy was going to be released.

"Can Toni and Kathy stay at our house for tonight?" I asked.

"I was going to suggest that since no one seems to be home at their place."

So we took them home with us.

"Is the guest room in order?" Dad asked Mom. "We've got a very comfortable double bed in there," he explained to the girls.

They looked so fragile and vulnerable as I led them upstairs. After I got them settled, I went back down to talk to my parents. Ailene had also joined them.

"Val, the doctor thinks that Kathy was beaten. He intends to report the case as possible child abuse. Do you know anything about their father?"

"Only that there have been problems. Toni said her mother left something like six years ago. Her brother went off and joined the army about two years ago. She's been taking care of Kathy and seeing to the house ever since. I've been worried their father was hitting Toni. I didn't know about Kathy."

"We shouldn't be involved in this," Mother said, wringing her delicate hands. "It's none of our business."

"Would you put them back in the same house again, not knowing what the situation is?" Dad countered.

"Legally, that man has every right to have his children with him," Mother warned.

"Legally, I'm not certain. Morally, I know he doesn't. Something has to be done for these children. We'll have to talk to them tomorrow, Val," he said, turning back to me.

"How awful," Ailene said. "I know things like that happen, but it's difficult to believe when it's someone you know."

ഌൟൟ

After breakfast on Saturday morning, I took Toni aside. It wasn't difficult because Ailene was busy giving Kathy the grand tour of her closet, which could last for hours.

"You've got to tell me the truth," I said.

Toni lowered her large, sad eyes. "It was an accident."

"No, it wasn't! You've got to tell the truth, or no one can help you."

Her cheeks flushed. "He didn't mean to do it."

I couldn't believe what I was hearing. How could she show loyalty to a parent who obviously didn't deserve it? "You don't really care about Kathy, do you?"

Toni began to sob. The tears were running down her face. "He has this drinking problem. He's really a good person when he's not drinking, but it's gotten worse lately. He can't seem to control it. Then he gets fired and has trouble getting another job, and the problem just gets worse. It was really my fault last night. I didn't want to give him my paycheck. I told him I needed the money to pay bills. We were arguing. Kathy doesn't normally get involved. He hits me but never her. This time, she got in the way. She tried to get him to stop, and he—" She couldn't get any more words out.

"Don't you want to protect her? Do you want her hurt again?"

Toni choked back a sob. "No! I love her! We need to stay together. Don't you see? We have to put up with it. They'll put us in foster care. They'll take her away from me. What other choices are there?"

"I don't know," I admitted, "but we could find out. No one should have to live this way. I think your father needs help too. You said he used to be a good person. Maybe he could be again if he got help sobering up. Don't you see, Toni, that it's wrong to keep a secret like this?"

She didn't answer me. She just sat there looking frightened.

"Anyway, that doctor is going to report it. So the matter's really out of our hands now."

I found my father and mother talking together in the kitchen. I told them exactly what Toni and I had discussed.

"I believe we're going to be contacted by a child welfare agency, the Division of Youth and Family Services," he explained to me. "We'll have to tell them everything we know. It may be a police matter as well."

I looked at my father in surprise. "You mean they could arrest Mr. Walker?"

His face wore a grave expression. "It's possible," he said, "I can't really say. But don't mention that to Toni right now because we don't really know anything. That doctor promised to get back to me. Meantime, encourage your friend to stay here for the weekend until something is clearly resolved. We can't let the girls go back there."

I agreed and returned to Toni. "My parents want you to stay for the weekend."

"No," she said. "My father will be home by now. He'll want us with him. He's probably getting worried. I'm sure he's really sorry about what he did."

"Just tell him you're with friends and let it go at that." I left the rec room while she called home.

The rest of the day went by quietly enough. Dad worked on repairing a broken grandfather clock he'd inherited from his father while Mom went to her health club. Ailene and I took Toni to the supermarket so she wouldn't have to miss work. While we were there, Kathy helped us do some food shopping for our house. Ailene even stopped and bought Kathy an ice cream cone on the way home as a reward. Kathy seemed to be recovering from what happened more quickly than we were.

At seven in the evening, my parents left the house all dressed up and ready for a night out. Mother left the number of their friends, the Collingwoods, just in case. Ailene immediately went to our phone after they left. She was still playing her little game, and I hated it.

Ray arrived at seven-thirty in full motorcycle regalia. "So how's it going?"

I decided not to tell him about Kathy. For some reason, I didn't think it was right. I felt it would in some way betray Toni. She and Kathy were upstairs, and maybe it was best if they didn't have to talk with Ray right now.

"School will be finished for the year soon. You got plans for the summer?"

I knew Ray was just trying to make polite small talk

until Ailene came down, but I actually enjoyed his company. His particular combination of rough-edged male friendliness and wry intelligence was appealing. Usually, he didn't take himself too seriously the way most people did.

Ailene finally came into the room looking stunning as usual. "Where do you want to go?" she asked Ray.

"Time you met some of my friends," he said. "Are you game?"

She smiled. "Are they very different?"

"Than you're used to? Yeah, I think so. I'm going to take you to a place called Billie's. Sometimes, it gets rowdy, but the place has atmosphere. Better wear your leather jacket tonight."

I got bad vibes about this. I wanted to tell Ailene not to go, yet I knew she'd never listen to me. A short time after they left, there was a knock at the door. I went to answer it and was surprised by the visitor.

Chapter 13

Jim was standing at our front door. We didn't exchange greetings because his eyes said it all.

"She's not here," I told him flatly.

"Where is she?"

I hesitated. "Why don't you come in?" I led him into the family room where Toni and Kathy were watching some dumb game show on TV.

We made small talk for a few minutes, but there was no putting him off. It seemed as if Ailene had become an obsession with him. I thought there was probably a fine line between love and insanity.

"You know stuff, Val. What's going on with Ailene? You've got to tell me! I need to talk to her again."

"Don't you see, Jimmy? The more passionate you get, the more you frighten her away. Sometimes to keep someone, you have to let them go."

"That sounds awesome deep," he said, "but I don't

think it's true. She's out with that low-life Zanka, isn't she?"

"He's not a low-life," Toni said heatedly. Clearly, she'd overheard our conversation.

Jim moved around so he could put us both in his line of vision. "So she is out with him again? Where'd they go?"

I shrugged uneasily. I'd never seen him in such an ugly mood. "Just some place that he usually goes to meet his friends."

Big mistake telling him, I realized too late. Jimmy seemed to swell with rage.

His body tensed. "What kind of place?"

"Billie's," I responded quietly.

"I've heard of that dump. It's a bar, a hang-out for bikers. Why would he take her to a sleazy place like that? It's somewhere in Crawfords Beach, isn't it?"

"Yes, on Front Street not far from the water," Toni said.

"You know where it is? Would you give me directions?"

"You can't go there," I exclaimed. "They're on a date. You can't interfere."

"Yes, I can." Jim's eyes shot sparks in my direction. "That place has a reputation. There are constant brawls, and the worst kinds of people hang out there. He had no right taking her there! It's not a fit place for a girl like Ailene—and not safe! I'm going to get her out of there!"

I could see there was no reasoning with him. He was a bundle of concentrated emotion. "I'll come along then," I said. I had this really bad feeling about the whole thing. I knew I couldn't stop Jimmy from going over there, but maybe I could cool it a little.

"I'll go too," Toni said.

Toni told Kathy not to answer the door while we were gone and she double-checked that the front door was locked. Then we took off with Jimmy in his Ford sedan, a sturdy, conservative car. We were all kind of tense and didn't do much talking. Toni just gave directions as Jim needed them.

Just as Jimmy said, Billie's looked like a real dump. It was about three blocks from the water, and for a scenic view, it faced an empty lot which had garbage and beer bottles strewn around. Jimmy was right: this wasn't Ailene's sort of environment—or mine, for that matter.

"Stay in the car," he ordered, "and keep the doors locked." Then he went inside.

I had no intention of listening to him. I followed him into the bar, hoping that no one would notice an underage kid. It was smoky, noisy, and crowded. No one did notice me at first. The place was crawling with guys in black leather motorcycle regalia. Beer drinking seemed to be the order of the day. I spotted Jimmy easily because he was one of the tallest in the room.

Ailene and Ray were seated at a table with another couple. The guy sitting with Ray had a shaved head and a dragon tattoo running down his neck. He looked seriously scary. Jimmy walked right up and began talking to them. I pushed my way across the room so I could get close.

"This isn't a safe place for you, Ailene," I could hear Jimmy say in a loud voice. "I'm taking you home."

"No, you're not," she said indignantly. "Stop stalking me. I'm here with friends. Please leave me alone."

But he wouldn't: his hand reached down and pulled at hers. Ray got to his feet. He was several inches shorter than Jim, but his build was broader and more powerful.

"Look, Ailene asked you to leave nice and polite. Quit bothering her."

Jimmy stood there looking down at Ray, not budging an inch.

I figured it was time for me to run interference. "Jim, I think we should go." Everyone stared at me.

"What are you doing here?" Ailene screeched, practically deafening me, even over the loud music playing in the background.

"Outside," Ray said with authority. "You're too young to be in here."

"Well, so is Ailene, and technically so are you," I pointed out.

"Let's settle this outside," Ray repeated, shrugging into his black leather jacket like a knight putting on armor for battle.

We all left Billie's, which didn't sadden me a bit. As soon as we were in front of the place, Jimmy tried to take Ailene's arm again, and she snatched it away.

"Jimmy, please, can't you see I don't want to go with you? I don't need a protector. I'm with Ray."

"What are you doing to yourself, Ailene? What are you doing to us?"

"There is no *us* anymore." She tried to turn her back on Jim at the same time he tried to pull her around to face him.

Ray moved between them. "Look, fella, Ailene is with me. Leave her alone. Stop stalking her." His voice was fierce but controlled. "I've tried to be patient with you. I'm asking you politely one last time to get out of here and not bother her anymore."

Jimmy lifted his chin combatively. He brought up his fist and tried to punch Ray in the jaw, but Ray had very quick reflexes. He used his leg in a karate move to sweep around and kick Jim off-balance, then Ray stepped away. I believe he hoped that would be the end of it. You could see he didn't want to hurt Jimmy. But Jim lunged at him again.

With one powerful arm, Ray blocked Jimmy's blow, and the other hand became a fist that caught Jim in the mid-section. Jimmy ended up doubled over on the ground, reminding me of the boy Ray had decked at the amuse-ment park.

Ailene was trembling. She turned to Ray. "Let's go," she said. "I really can't stand this." She turned to me then. "Make sure he's all right."

She bent and touched Jimmy's face lightly with her fingertips and then hurried away. I couldn't tell, but I thought she might have been fighting back tears.

As I tried to help Jimmy to his feet, we heard the rum-ble of a motorcycle starting. I could see them disappear-ing into the distance as we hobbled back to the car.

"God, I feel like I've been stomped by an elephant,"

Jim said, barely catching his breath. "I really made my-self look like a fool in front of Ailene, didn't I?"

There wasn't much point in answering. Toni had seen the whole thing from the car, so she kept silent as well.

"Are you all right?" I asked.

"I guess I'm going to be sore for a few days," he said, grinding down on his back teeth.

"Maybe you ought to see a doctor."

He shook his head fiercely. "I've gotten worse done to me in football games. Don't worry, I'm fine. But I shouldn't have let him get the best of me. Now I've lost her forever!"

Jimmy brooded the entire way home, running his left hand distractedly through his short-cropped sandy hair as he drove. I could practically smell the misery in his soul. He dropped us off in front of my house and then drove away without another word. I couldn't help but wish that somebody someday would love me as much as Jim loved Ailene.

"I think he'll be okay, physically anyhow," I said to Toni.

"Jimmy really is special, but he just doesn't measure up to Ray." Toni sighed deeply. There was no misunder-standing that sigh. It was the expression of an all-consuming crush.

Kathy was very glad to see us return. It had to be at least a little bit scary for her, being in a big, strange house with no one around.

Around nine o'clock, we were watching some boring television repeats—punishment for people who didn't have anywhere to go on Saturday night—when the telephone rang. I answered it after the first ring. It turned out to be Toni's father. Since he asked for her, I handed over the phone. He did most of the talking, and she started looking upset.

"No, Dad, please don't come here. Kathy and I are staying for the weekend like I told you before." Then she hung up.

"You told him where you were?" I asked in surprise.

"I only told him who I was with, but I have your telephone number and address in a little book I keep by the phone. He must have gone through it. He said he's coming over to get us. I don't want you to have any trouble on our account. I think Kathy and I better go with him." I saw that familiar frightened look come over Toni's face again.

"Hey, this is my house. He can't just bust in here and grab away my guests." I spoke with more bravado than I felt.

"Thanks, Val, but you don't need to be involved in our problems." She lowered her head, her hair falling forward, and I thought how much Toni reminded me of a willow tree bending to weep in the wind.

"I'm very much involved," I said. What should I do? Call my parents? I hated to ruin their evening. Besides, Dad said they weren't going to be home late. If Mr. Walker did come by, there was no reason why we had to let him in. If necessary, I could always call the police. He might have his own children scared to death, but he wasn't going to intimidate me.

For all my fine resolve, when I heard someone at the front door around nine-thirty, I must have jumped three miles in the air. It turned out to be Ailene and Ray. I was glad to see them and breathed a sigh of relief. Ailene invited Ray in for a while which delighted Kathy and, I believe, Toni as well, although she wasn't as open about it.

"So how were the drinks at Billie's?" I asked.

Ailene wrinkled her up-turned nose in my direction. "I had ginger ale, if you must know," she said.

"Sure you did!"

"For real," she said. "You know I don't have a fake ID."

I wouldn't question Ray, and I doubted a bartender would either. He looked a lot older than his actual age.

"Was Jimmy all right?" Ailene seemed genuinely concerned.

"His pride was more bruised than anything else," I reassured her.

A funny look came over her, as if she too were in pain. "I'll go fix us something," she told Ray. She left us quickly and went out to the kitchen.

Ray sat down next to Kathy on the couch. He looked down at her arm. "How'd you do that?"

Kathy looked over at Toni as if to ask permission to speak. Toni nodded her head, indicating it was all right for her to talk to him.

"Daddy sort of hit me, but Toni says he didn't mean to hurt me. He gets sick sometimes. You know, like mixed up, and then he doesn't know what he's doing. But he's always sorry later."

Ray patted her head gently. His face held a grim expression, and his dark, bottomless eyes were impossible to read. I thought he must be thinking of his own father.

It amazed me how loyal both girls were to their dad. I thought about my own father. He had hit me exactly once in my life. I remember the incident vividly. In fact, it was my first memory. I was about three years old. Mom was trying to give me some kind of yucky liquid medicine because I was sick. Me being me, I wouldn't take it. I refused to let her force it down my gullet. I remember knocking the spoon with the medicine in it on the kitchen floor.

That was when she yelled for Dad. When he came, she told him to make me take the medicine.

"Spank her! She's got to be punished. She has to learn to obey us."

Dad took another spoon of medicine and tried to make me swallow it. When I still refused, he put me over his knee and paddled me once. I kept on yelling "*No!*" at the top of my lungs. So he hit me again, and I still refused. By the time he'd paddled me four times, he was just as upset as I was. Tears welled in his eyes. It was the only time I ever saw him look that way.

"Jan, she won't take it. I'm never hitting her again. It's stupid, and it doesn't solve anything."

He started to walk away, and I remember going after him, tugging at his sleeve, and begging him not to cry, that I would be good and take the medicine.

I realized that, even if my father did love Ailene more, he had always been kind to me. I could trust him. There was no brutality in the man. I wondered what would have happened to me if I had Mr. Walker for a father. I shuddered.

"You in much pain?" Ray asked Kathy.

Funny, you wouldn't think someone like Ray could be as compassionate and caring as he was with Kathy and Toni. But then appearances were often deceiving.

"I'm better now," Kathy said. She cast her eyes downward like she was ashamed of what had happened to her, as if she blamed herself.

I seated myself on the sofa at Ray's left side. Kathy was beside him on the right and Toni next to her.

Kathy raised her face toward him like a flower to the sun. "Ray, would a younger woman have a chance with you?"

After registering momentary surprise, Ray flashed his easy smile. He seemed genuinely touched. He took Kathy's small hand in his huge, work-roughened one that never completely lost the grime of auto engines. "I used to be a friend of your brother before he went away. Bet you miss him. Suppose you think of me the way you did Eddy? And maybe I can be like a brother to you until yours comes home. Would that be okay?"

Kathy smiled happily and then gave Ray an ardent hug.

"Hey, what's this," Ailene said, returning with a tray of lemonade glasses. Her lips formed a perfect smile. "Do I have competition for this man?"

"Wonderful as you are, doll, I do enjoy having my harem of admirers," he responded with his own teasing smile.

Kathy giggled with delight as Ray reached over and engulfed all three of us sitting with him in an enormous but oddly gentle bear hug.

"You certainly are a lady killer," Ailene retorted.

"But I fought for you tonight," he pointed out, intently staring as if trying to read her thoughts.

"That you did," she said, a shadow crossing her lovely face.

We enjoyed the lemonade together for a time. Ray told us some humorous stories about work at the garage. Kathy listened worshipfully but finally started to yawn and look tired. Toni was just about to put Kathy to bed when the doorbell rang.

"I hope it's not Jimmy again," Ailene said with apparent anxiety. "He's so stubborn."

"Don't knock it. That bulldog determination is what makes him an outstanding athlete," Ray said.

Ailene looked surprised. "I didn't think you knew anything about Jimmy."

"Oh, I still follow high school sports in the local paper. I knew Jim Saunders once."

I recalled what Jimmy had told us about Ray and what a great athlete he was. "I'll see who it is," I said, remembering that it might very well be Mr. Walker. I called out cautiously and asked who it was.

The voice on the other side of the door was male, loud and belligerent. "It's Brock Walker. Let me in! I've come for my girls."

"Go away," I called through the door. "Toni and Kathy are staying here for the weekend."

"I'll smash in this door if you don't open up." He sounded out of control.

Toni came running forward. Her eyes had a haunted look. "It's no use. We have to go with him."

"Not when he's like that! He'll only start beating on both of you again. Next time it could be worse than a broken arm or some bruises."

"No, I'll talk to him." Toni pushed by me and opened the door before I could stop her. "Daddy, we want to stay with our friends until Monday."

Mr. Walker lumbered into the room, a big, beefy man with a red face and a beer belly.

I didn't like the look of the man at all. Of course, I admit, I hated him before I ever saw him.

"You're out of here," he said. "Get Kathy."

"Mr. Walker, maybe you didn't mean to do it, but you broke Kathy's arm, and you didn't even hang around long enough to find out how badly you hurt her."

"Who are you to talk to me that way?" His face was as red as a rare roast. His breath rivaled a distillery. He raised his hand as if to strike me.

At that moment, I felt strong hands moving me aside. Ray was suddenly eyeball to eyeball with Mr. Walker. "Look, go home and sleep it off! Your kids are perfectly safe here. They're with friends who really care about them."

"You're saying I don't care?" Mr. Walker angrily peered at us through bloodshot eyes. Ray put an arm on his and tried to guide the older man back to the door, but Mr. Walker pulled away, weaving toward Mother's snow-white living room. "Kathy, where are you, girl? Daddy's come for you."

Ray's eyes narrowed into bullets. "I'm asking you nicely to get out of here. This is a private house, and you've been told to leave."

Ailene came into the living room followed by Kathy. They said nothing. All eyes were turned on the confrontation between the two men.

"I don't know who you are, but you're in my way. I'm taking my girls and then I'm leaving." He turned to Toni furiously. "And you have some explaining to do when we get home. These strangers shouldn't know our business."

"Please, Dad, I did what I thought was best. Let Kathy stay here. I'll go with you."

Suddenly, he seemed to lose it completely. His eyes smoldered like glowing coals. He grabbed Toni's arm, squeezing it hard, and when she cried out and tried to pull away, he slapped her.

I suppose it was more than Ray could stand. He punched Walker in the face, and the man went down, blood spurting from his nose.

"I know your kind," Ray said, pinning Walker with a hard, dangerous look. "You make me sick! You beat up on helpless women and children because it makes you feel like a man. But you're not a man. You can't even face up to one. You're nothing but garbage, a pathetic bully and a mean drunk. Get up, you coward! Let your children see you for the slime you really are."

"You broke my nose!" Walker moaned then started to blubber in drunken abandonment.

Ray backed off in disgust. Ailene recoiled, running from the room.

"I'll do worse to you if I ever hear that you touch them again. Understand? I'll be keeping an eye on both of them from now on."

Walker made a movement as if to lift himself from the floor. Ray raised his fist. Toni ran toward him, tears streaming down her face. She hurled herself against Ray.

"No, please, don't hit him again," she sobbed, clinging to Ray, her hands fastened tightly against his muscled arms. Ray relaxed his fists, putting one arm around Toni's shoulder as if to comfort her. With the other, he stroked her long, dark hair in a calming gesture. They could have been the only two people on the face of the earth, the communication between them was that private and total.

"You have to understand, I can't let him hurt you anymore," he told her in a now-controlled tone of voice.

Walker fell back inertly and lay still.

"He's still my father."

"I guess for a minute there, I confused him with mine," Ray mused. They were lost in the misery they had in common.

"What's going on here?" I was startled by my father's voice. My parents were standing in the hall.

"Mr. Walker was just leaving," Ray said.

"I got a right to have my children," Walker said, slurring his words. His belligerence had diminished dramatically.

My father helped the man to his feet and handed him a handkerchief for his nose. "You won't be getting these children back if I have anything to do with it," Dad told him. Then he escorted Mr. Walker into the hall.

My mother let out a horrified cry, and we all looked at her. "There's blood all over my white carpet!"

"I'll get it out," I promised unemotionally.

"Sorry about the stains on the rug," Ray apologized, "but I couldn't let him hurt the girls. My old man was a lot like him. You can't give in to a bully. There's only one thing they understand—fear."

Dad regarded Ray gravely. "I think there are other ways to deal with people like him, proper legal channels."

"Sir, you don't have to agree, but it's been my experience that people confuse kindness for weakness."

"I'll be calling the police now," Dad said. "They're better equipped to deal with this kind of thing than we are."

"Don't do that. I'm gonna leave," Mr. Walker said, coming toward Dad. "I'll be back for my girls tomorrow."

"No, you can't drive a car in the condition you're in," Dad said. "You were lucky not to have an accident driving over here."

My father called the cops just as he said he would and kept Mr. Walker with him until they arrived. Mr. Walker didn't have any fight left in him, so detaining him wasn't any problem for my father.

Dad explained what had happened to the police officers. He described Ray's behavior in heroic terms. After the two patrolmen wrote out their report, they took Mr. Walker into custody. He made some nasty threats against all of us as he left, and we were glad to see the last of him for the time being.

Ailene had returned to the room by then. She noticed the blood on Ray's hand and averted her gaze. Her face lost all color.

After my parents and Kathy had gone upstairs, Toni spoke to Ray. "Thank you for helping us."

He smiled down at her, their eyes making contact. "I meant what I said to your old man. I intend to watch out for you and your sister from now on." As Toni slowly walked upstairs, Ray's eyes followed her with a look I couldn't quite read.

I slipped into the rec room, closed my eyes, and rested in the dark. It had been a nerve-wracking evening. I could hear Ailene and Ray talking in the living room. Besides me, they were the only ones left downstairs.

"I hate it when you're violent. It really turns me off."

"Walker is a child abuser and who knows what else? Don't tell me you're upset because I hit him." I could hear the hurt and indignation in Ray's voice. "I like you a lot, Ailene, but I don't understand the way you think."

"You and I are very different."

"I thought that was what you liked about me."

"I never said you weren't attractive, but there are things about you that frighten me."

"Like?"

"You have a bad temper."

"I've never hit a woman. I never will. And I never started a fight in my life."

"Being with you is like trying to hold lightning in my hand. It's dangerous and scary."

"But exciting?"

"Maybe. At first, I thought it was, but Ray, it isn't working. I just don't think we're right for each other."

"If you want me to come begging to you the way Saunders did, forget it! I don't beg! Was it that stuff with him that changed your mind about me? No, you don't have to answer that. You probably don't know anyway. I think you've still got some growing up to do. You're a little mixed up in your head. It's all right. I understand. See you around, Ailene."

I heard the front door slam followed by the sound of sobbing. *Déjà vu.* Quietly, I went to the kitchen and heated up some warm milk. She was there, still crying in the living room when I returned with the milk. She shook her head when I offered it to her.

"I don't want any," she said. Her eyes were puffy, and her nose had reddened.

"Better have some. We read in science once how milk has something in it that calms the nerves naturally. It's good stuff."

I guess she was too worn out to argue with me any further because she took the milk and drank it down at a single gulp. "Ray's right, my head is all messed up."

"Let's talk tomorrow."

She nodded and went wearily upstairs. I got some cleanser and cloths then began working on the bloodstains. *Out, out, damn spot.* So much for my knowledge of Shakespeare.

Chapter 14

Our telephone rang at eleven o'clock the next morning, breaking the tranquility of our Sunday the way a careless child shatters a glass jar. I was the one nearest the phone, and so I took the call. It turned out to be Dave.

"You sound surprised to hear from me," he said.

"I just wasn't thinking about you."

"Thanks a bunch."

"A lot's been happening around here lately."

"Such as?"

I looked around. I was alone in the family room. Ailene was still upstairs, and everyone else was having breakfast in the kitchen. "Ailene broke up with Ray last night. He and Jimmy got into a fight over her. I think she's through with both of them."

"Yes!" Dave shouted in exultation. "I'll be right over!"

"Now?"

"Sure, why not?"

"Because Ailene is very vulnerable at this moment."

"That's the whole idea. This is just what I've been waiting for."

"Why don't you wait a couple of days?"

"Do you know how little time is left until the prom? Besides, it's time I made my own luck. Wasn't it Napoleon who said that luck is what happens when preparation meets opportunity?"

"Probably before Waterloo."

"One other thing, Val. Will you talk to her before I get there? Tell her some nice things about me, and how much I like her. Soften her up."

"I'd rather not. You're a vulture."

"Hey, you owe me. Come on, be a friend!"

There was a click at the other end. I just sat there for several minutes staring off into space. He was right, I had promised to help him, but I really wished I hadn't. With a deep sigh, I slowly climbed the stairs to Ailene's room. I knocked at the door, and she called out to come in. She was still lying in bed with the shades drawn. I pulled up the shades, never being one to accept the dark if I don't have to, and then I sat down at the foot of her bed.

"Dave Greene just phoned. He's coming over to talk to you."

She looked surprised. "Talk to me about what?"

"He wants to ask you to the senior prom. It's the dream of his life. In fact, it's practically a monomania with him. Just call him Ahab."

"I had no idea."

"He says he's had a crush on you since kindergarten."

"How sweet," she said with a smile.

"Are you going to accept?"

"Of course not."

"Why not?" I asked.

She sat up in her bed. "I don't think I'm going to date anyone for a while."

"Because of yesterday?"

"Partly. I need time to get my head together. I don't want to hurt anyone else. It just seems like I don't know what I want anymore. I'm really conflicted and confused."

I noticed an open book on the nightstand and glanced at it. It was her copy of the works of Ralph Waldo Emerson. We'd read some of his transcendental essays in English class.

I glanced at the words Ailene had underlined: *The virtue in most request is conformity. Self-reliance is its aversion...Whoso would be a man must be a non-conformist.*

"Are you worried about being too much of a conformist?" I was trying very hard to understand her.

"Sure, that's part of it. I've got to find out who and what I am. I'm tired of going out with guys who only see me as pretty and popular, and expect a blonde airhead."

"You're no bubble brain. Anyone who knows you would never think so. But, Ailene, you are pretty and popular. What's wrong with that?"

"Suppose they never see beyond it?"

"You think Jimmy is like that?"

She nodded her head miserably. "All he ever seemed to say to me was how beautiful I was. Maybe that's all he noticed about me."

"But you two seemed so perfect for each other. Maybe that's what he thought you wanted to hear."

"That's society's view of things."

"Sometimes society is right."

"I think Jimmy just sees me as another trophy for his showcase." Ailene got out of bed and threw a robe around the silky blue nightgown that complimented her eyes. "Even Ray never saw past my looks. Sometimes I think beauty is a curse! You can never be sure people love you for yourself. And what happens when beauty fades? Will I have to spend my entire life worrying about maintaining my looks?" I could hear her unspoken "like Mother" as loudly as if she had actually said it.

"If beauty is a curse then let me be hexed."

Ailene turned and looked at me, tilting her head sideways in appraisal. "You've got nice features, Val. A little make-up wouldn't hurt, and you need to do something with your hair rather than just letting it hang the way it does. You may be kind of skinny, but you'll fill out in time. With a little effort, you can really be attractive. Most girls can if they just pay some attention to their looks. Tell you what—if you like, I'll help you."

"Would you?"

She smiled at me warmly. "Sure, we're sisters, aren't we? And the one thing I really know about is keeping up appearances."

With a sudden burst of feeling, I leaned over and hugged her. "Seems as if looks are getting more important to me and less important to you." I was thoughtful for a moment. "Maybe Dave would be good for you. He is a cerebral guy. Maybe that's what you need."

"Quite frankly, Dave Greene is a little short for me. You know how dumb we'd look together at the prom? I hate wearing flats, but even if I did wear them, he'd still be vertically challenged. People would mock us."

"I thought you decided that you're a non-conformist, and looks aren't so important anymore. Didn't you just tell me it's what a person is like on the inside that matters?"

She stared at me. "You really are growing up."

"It just seems hypocritical to criticize guys for valuing looks most when, deep down, you feel the same way about them."

"I suppose you're right," she agreed, tilting her head to one side. "Listen, you go downstairs and wait for Dave. I've got to get dressed."

I left her rummaging through her closet, and went to check on Toni and Kathy. I found them both in a quiet, tense mood, and I knew they were concerned about what was going to happen to them and their father. I didn't try to discuss it with them because I didn't really know either.

My dad was right: they couldn't go home again, not when home meant being subjected to beatings from a drunk. I knew my father would make sure they were properly cared for. We could trust him to do what was right.

I let a very excited Dave in the front door a few minutes later. "Did you talk to her?" he asked eagerly. "Did you build me up in her eyes?"

"Today really isn't a good time. Why don't you wait to talk to her about the prom?"

"No, I feel it in my bones! My time has come! Where is she?" His eyes were bright, his cheeks flushed as if fevered.

"She'll be down in a few minutes. Just one thing, she could refuse you. What will you do then?"

He shook his head, and that uncooperative lock of hair fell across his forehead. "I can't think about losing. It's like taking a test. I study hard, do all the necessary preparation. Then I go in there confident, ready to ace it."

"This isn't school, and Ailene isn't a test score. She's a human being. She still says she doesn't want to go to the prom. In fact, right now, she doesn't feel like dating any boy."

"Only because she hasn't been involved with the right one." He walked past me. "No more negative thinking."

Dave was warmly received by my parents, particularly my mother. Then Ailene walked into the family room. She was wearing a yellow sundress, and with her golden hair catching the sunlight, she looked like a glorious marigold. Maybe beauty was Ailene's curse as she thought it was, but it was not without its advantages. Dave couldn't take his eyes off her. He stood there mesmerized, staring in frank admiration.

"Val said you wanted to talk with me?"

He cleared his throat nervously. "Can we go for a walk or something?"

"Sure. Whatever." They left the house together.

"What do you think he wants to ask her?" Mother inquired.

"To go with him to the senior prom. He's been planning it for quite a while." Even to me, my voice sounded flat.

Mother, of course, didn't notice and glowed with pleasure. "How wonderful! Do you think she'll accept?"

I told her that I didn't know and then tried to pick out part of the newspaper to read. But I couldn't concentrate. Why should I care? Maybe I did have some feelings for Dave, but wasn't it stupid? Dave didn't see me for dirt! All he ever thought about was Ailene. Even if she did refuse him, he'd always want her, not me.

I stood up and began pacing back and forth in front of the fireplace.

"Dear, why don't you go for a jog or something? You're going to wear out the carpet." Mother viewed me with disdain.

"Great idea, anyone want to come with me?"

Toni offered, and I took her up on it.

"Nice day for a walk," I said. Toni kept up with my brisk pace, and we didn't do much talking. We were both preoccupied with our own problems. Hers were a lot more serious than mine, and I felt guilty even comparing them. But I was hurting too.

"Do you think we'll ever see Ray again?" she asked, suddenly stopping.

Her question surprised me a little. "I get the feeling he really cares about you and Kathy."

"Like he does about his sisters?" The velvet glow of her violet eyes grew dusky, sorrowful.

"He might think of Kathy like a sister, but I don't think he feels that way about you."

"He's so hot. I hope you're right."

"I'm a regular Dear Abby when it comes to understanding other people's problems," I assured her.

"Maybe there might be a chance he would come to really care about me?"

"Just give it some time."

"I'm a very patient person." She sighed. "Anyway, I have other more pressing concerns. Kathy had nightmares last night," Toni said in a quiet, worried voice.

"I'm not surprised."

"I'm frightened too. I mean, bad as things got, we were always still a family. Even after Mom and Eddy left, there was the three of us. Now I don't know what's going to happen." Toni's voice was choked. She looked as if she were fighting back tears.

"Maybe it'll force your father to get counseling. Then you could be a real family again."

Toni nodded. "I wish I had a family like yours."

I don't know why that surprised me, but it did. I never thought about how Toni must see us. "Things aren't so great with us either. My mother's never hit me, but she's a master of verbal torture."

My mother once asked me why I chose Toni for a friend. Now I finally had a clue. It dawned on me that I had recognized a kindred spirit in her, someone who knew about suffering. Toni blamed herself for the way her father treated her. I always thought I was no good because that was what my mother implied. Neither one of us thought much of ourselves.

Now I was fighting back against my situation, trying to be helpful to other people, maybe to convince myself that my mother was wrong about me. I discovered that doing things for others did make me feel a lot better about myself. As for Toni, she had to be made to see that she was not to blame for her father's problems, nor could she solve them by herself.

When we got back to the house, Ailene and Dave were standing together in the driveway. They turned to us.

"Val, I want you to be the first to know that Ailene is going to be my date for the prom." Dave's face was flushed with victory.

Ailene stood oddly still beside him.

I felt a lump form in my throat and turned to my sister. "How come? I mean, I thought you weren't going because it was the conformist thing to do."

"Well, you really convinced me. The old Ailene would never have considered going with Dave. I was so superficial, so shallow. Fortunately, Dave is above that sort of thing."

"Is he? Well, have a great time together."

"Stay for lunch?" Ailene asked Dave.

"Love it," he said, offering her his arm.

I was the one who convinced Ailene to go to the prom with Dave? How stupid can one person be? I decided to go to the kitchen and OD on chocolate chip cookies. At least I would die happy. Except before I got there, my appetite deserted me. I walked into the house with Toni. Ailene and Dave had gone ahead of us. Dave was telling my parents his news, and I could hear Mom congratulating both of them. She was chirping like a bird.

"No one should ever miss the senior prom! It's so special, an event you'll remember and treasure for your entire life."

"Prom is derived from the word promenade," Dave said.

"Fascinating," Mother responded.

The old me would have commented that no one really cared, but I was determined to avoid sarcasm.

"Dave, I'm so glad you convinced Ailene to change her mind about going." Mother gushed on and on. She acted like they were practically engaged. It was nauseating. I couldn't stay in the room.

I went back outside and sat down on the white wrought iron bench under the porch columns, wanting to be alone. Except I hadn't been out there very long when a car pulled up to the house and out stepped Jimmy Saunders.

He walked up the stone pathway that cut through the lawn and sat down beside me on the bench.

"Didn't think you'd ever come back."

"Only to apologize for how I behaved yesterday. I'm ashamed of myself. I let my feelings get the best of me."

"I guess we all do that sometimes." Wasn't I doing that right now? "She's not angry at you anymore."

"She's not?" He looked hopeful.

"She broke up with Ray last night."

His eyes were riveted to mine. "Because of me?"

"Maybe. Ray thought so. But I don't know. They really weren't suited to each other. I think she finally realized it."

"I'm going to try to patch it with her one last time."

I touched his arm. "I better tell you that Dave Greene is here."

"So?"

"So he asked her to be his date to the prom, and she accepted."

"I don't believe it! She's going with *him*? What's wrong with her? She must really hate me."

"Ailene thinks you only want her because she's pretty and popular, that you don't really care about her for herself."

"That's so outrageous. I can't even believe she thinks that way."

"Well, she does. You'll have to find a way to convince her that your attraction to her is more than physical. Otherwise, forget it. Look, I'll try to get her to talk to you. Maybe the two of you can finally sort things out."

"Thanks, Val, you're a real friend."

"That's me, everybody's pal." I wondered how I'd look with angel wings.

I walked inside the house and located Ailene in the rec room with the family. "I need to talk with you privately for a few minutes," I said.

My parents looked at me questioningly, but I quickly led Ailene from the room before they could say anything.

Out in the front hall, Ailene turned to me. "What is it?"

Afraid Mom might call the police if she knew Jim was lurking outside, I insisted Ailene go upstairs to her room with me for a private conversation. "Jimmy's here," I told her.

She frowned deeply and looked upset. "Tell him to go away. It's all been said before."

"Not everything. Ailene, I've got one question for you."

"What's that?"

"I'm not a big brain like Dave, but it seems to me that a person could appear to be a conformist and still be an individual. What I mean is, suppose you happened to like the way things are, the status quo?"

She blinked at me. "I don't understand, Val."

"Suppose you enjoyed being pretty and popular, being a top student, and having terrific guys admire you? What's so wrong with that? Does it mean you're a conformist if you're doing what makes you happy?"

She bit her lower lip thoughtfully. "I guess not."

"I'm not trying to tell you what to do. It probably sounds like I'm attempting to manipulate you, but that isn't really it at all. I think you've got to stand up for what you believe, no matter what other people think— good or bad. There were an awful lot of people who thought I was a pain, but everyone's different. It seems to me that since you broke up with Jimmy, you've been pretty miserable. What I'm trying to say, and not saying very well, is that you ought to follow your own heart and do what makes you happy. I can't really tell you what that is, and neither can Mom or Dad. But you ought not to do things just to prove you're a non-conformist. Being different is fine for some people. Maybe it just doesn't suit you. You're never going to please everyone, so just do what's best for yourself. Am I making any sense?"

Ailene smiled at me. "You're making lots of sense. I never realized how smart you are." She gave me a hug. "As sisters go, I guess I could do worse."

"The thing is I never understood why you changed in the first place. I mean you always seemed like the most together person I've ever known." Had my wish brought all the trouble into her life? I still couldn't bring myself to tell her what I had done. I knew it was cowardly, but she was just starting to accept me. I didn't want to ruin our new connection as sisters.

Ailene's eyes darkened. Then she faced me squarely. "If I tell you something, promise you'll never tell Dad? Because it would only hurt him. Can I trust you with an important secret?"

I nodded my head gravely. "Honor bright."

For a moment, she frowned, looking deeply into my eyes, into my soul. Her voice was a soft whisper when she spoke. "Mom had a boyfriend."

"What?" I couldn't have been more shocked. "No! She couldn't!"

"It's true. I didn't want to believe it either, but I over-heard her talking to him on the phone one day when she didn't know I was home." Her eyes never left mine, as if she wanted to hold me together with them in case I fractured.

"How could she? Who?" I could hardly catch my breath.

"Some guy from work, I think."

"Shouldn't Dad know? Does he?" My chest felt very tight.

"No, I don't think he knows, and no, he shouldn't. Besides, I think it's over. I heard her telling him so on the phone that day. I think that's why he called the house, because he didn't accept it. I slipped out quietly, so she never even knew I was there."

"I would have confronted her with it."

Ailene laughed without mirth. "Of course you would! That's why I wouldn't tell you. Don't you see? There isn't any point. The important thing is that I don't feel the same way about her anymore. I see her as she really is, a liar and a hypocrite. I don't want to end up being like her, and I'm afraid I am already a duplicate copy."

Any anger I felt toward my mother dissolved in the pity I felt for Ailene, for the pain and disillusionment she had suffered, for what she had tried to spare Dad and me.

"Maybe I shouldn't have told you," she said, obviously having second thoughts.

"No, I'm glad you did. And like you said, Mom did end it, so there's no reason for Dad to know unless she wants to tell him. But, Ailene, you're not like her, at least, not anymore."

"That's good, because I don't want to get to be her age and still only worry about how attractive people find me. She doesn't love Dad, not really. She loves being loved and admired, and I was her clone. It sickens me."

"I'm not going to defend her, but I guess she's got her own problems and insecurities to deal with. That's what Dad says."

We walked outside together. Jimmy was still sitting where I'd left him. He got up hurriedly when he saw Ailene. They just stood there looking at each other for a few seconds. Jimmy reached for Ailene's hand then thought better of it and stuck his hands in his jeans pockets.

"Val thinks I might have scared you away by becoming too intense and asking you to make a serious commitment to me. If that's the case, I'm sorry. I'll back off and let you have your space."

"I'm sorry too. I've been cruel to you."

"I acted like a jerk yesterday. I'm surprised you're even willing to speak to me."

She came closer to him. "No, I understand how you felt. You were very brave. And seeing you come after me that way, I realized how much you care."

"You have no idea how much." Jimmy shook with emotion. He put his arms around Ailene's shoulders. She reached out to him.

"Let's go talk in the backyard where it's private," Ailene suggested.

As I walked inside the house, I breathed a deep sigh. I was glad that they were reconciling.

Mother called out to me, and I went back to the rec room. "Where's Ailene?"

"She'll be here soon," I said.

"Good, because Dave is waiting for her."

I had forgotten all about him. He was there all right, and Ailene had promised to go to the prom with him. Ailene wasn't the type of person to break a promise, but she should be able to go with Jimmy if that was what she wanted. I went to the sliding glass door, moved back the curtain slightly, and looked out. There they were, Jimmy and Ailene in each other's arms, kissing with real feeling. I turned back to the others in the room.

"I have to talk to Dave privately," I said in a firm voice.

Mom and Dad exchanged looks. "We were about to put lunch together," Dad said. "Toni, maybe you and Kathy could give us a hand in the kitchen?" They left me alone with Dave.

"Please look outside in the yard for a moment." I drew back the curtain for him.

He stared in silence, his expression changing from one of self-satisfaction to desolation. Ailene and Jimmy were lost in each other's embrace. Dave couldn't fail to understand the implications.

"They talked out their problems. I don't think anyone should stand in the way of love, do you?"

"You told me yourself that Ailene doesn't know her own mind, let alone know what love is." He turned away from the glass.

"She was confused for a while, but she's pulling it all together now. They are right for each other. You know that just as well as I do." I watched him sit down on the couch, lowering his face between his hands. "She'll still go with you to the prom if you insist on it. Ailene doesn't give her word lightly. She's got integrity."

"Terrific, then there's really no problem."

"But you wouldn't say that if you truly cared about her. You'd be heartbroken the way Jimmy was when she wouldn't see him."

He stood up and confronted me angrily. "What are you saying?"

I glared right back at him. "That you don't care anything about her. She's just a symbol of success for you, like an A on a test. Except Ailene is a person, a sensitive human being, and she needs and deserves more."

"That's right, get in my face, why don't you? Make me out to be some kind of selfish creep. Isn't this around the time you generally call me a nerd or a geek?"

I shook my fist at him. "You're smart about school-work, but when it comes to understanding how people feel, you're really dumb. And where Ailene's concerned, you have been acting like a scavenger, a total vulture."

We were eyeball to eyeball now.

"That's exactly the kind of nasty remark I've come to expect from you. Well, let me tell you something, Miss Smart Mouth, you're not so terrific yourself, even if you obviously think you know it all."

I made an impetuous decision that I was afraid I'd live to regret. "Would you please take off your glasses?"

"Why, so you can punch me?"

I shoved him down on the couch. "No, so I can show you how I really feel about you and always have."

He took off his glasses, and, without stopping to think, I threw my arms around his neck and kissed him firmly on the lips. At first, he pulled back in surprise, but then, he took me in his arms and kissed me back with a hard smack. It was such an exciting moment for me I could hardly catch my breath. When we came apart, I had the impression that he felt the same way I did. He was looking at me strangely, as if he'd never seen me before.

"I always thought you hated me."

"I was just angry that you wanted Ailene and not me. I couldn't compete with her. I still can't."

"You don't have to." He took my hand and held it tightly. "You were so sarcastic and critical, I thought you couldn't stand me."

"I was hurt. I wanted you to like me. I was afraid to let myself be vulnerable to you."

We sat for a while, holding hands, not saying another word. It didn't seem necessary.

When Ailene and Jimmy came into the house, Dave went up to them. "Ailene, I hope you won't be offended. I've changed my mind about taking you to the prom. It would be a mistake for both of us. The fact is, I intend to ask Val if she'll go with me."

Ailene took his hand. "I understand, Dave," she said. She gave me a wink and gave him a hug.

When lunch was ready, we all sat down together at the dining room table. Dad seemed pleased, but Mother was particularly happy.

"Both my girls going to the senior prom. How lovely! And with such wonderful dates. We are going to have such fun shopping for dresses together, and I have the most divine new hairdresser!"

I rolled my eyes and groaned.

"Please, Mother, let's not discuss it," Ailene pressed her lips together as if to prevent herself from speaking further.

I could tell by the expression on her face that Mother's feelings were hurt. My father appeared to be aware of it too. He looked intently from Ailene to me. His eyes took on an expression I couldn't interpret.

"We'll talk later," Dad said in a compelling manner.

Chapter 15

The boys had gone home. Toni and Kathy were upstairs. Long shadows cast themselves across the rec room when Dad came and took my arm.

"Come on," he said.

"Where?"

"The living room." His voice had an assertiveness I'd never heard before.

I suppose I just stared at him in surprise. He went and got Mother and Ailene, steering them into the living room too.

"What's going on?" Mother asked.

"I said we needed to have a family conference, and I meant it." Then he ripped the clear plastic covers off the chairs and couch as Mother protested loudly. He moved with determination. "A living room is meant for a family to live in."

"We have the family room for that!"

"Sit down so we can talk. Jan, you've repeatedly asked me to take charge. Ray may have a point: people do confuse kindness for weakness. So I intend to be firm. Ailene has been very rude and disrespectful of late, and I expect that to end."

Mother sank down on the sofa. "Things are getting better with Ailene. I really don't see the need for this. Val, did you say something to your father?" She pointed a blood-red fingernail at me.

I shook my head at her. "You always do that, Mother, blame me, make me the scapegoat. No, I did not say anything to Dad."

"I'm sure you're lying."

Ailene rose to her feet. "Val's right. You do pick on her. And I'm ashamed to say I used to go right along with it."

"Fine, so it's blame Mother time." She faced Ailene angrily. "The unkindest cut of all!"

"Jan, you *are* unfair to Val."

Dad's accusation was too much for Mother. She began to tremble. "Val is willful and spiteful, and she's turned you both against me. I'm sorry I had a second child."

My fists clenched involuntarily, and my whole body went taut. Although what Mother said did not surprise me, I felt myself unable to speak. The old feelings of hurt and rejection returned. I looked away from her, fixing my eyes on the Lenox and Wedgwood pieces gracefully perched on the mantle.

"Why did you say that?" Dad asked Mother.

I glanced over at him, wondering how much disappointment I had caused him over the years.

"I didn't say it to be hurtful," Mother's voice seemed oddly lacking in emotion now.

"I don't see how you can be so cruel and then say you didn't mean to hurt! What planet are you from?" Ailene said, suddenly standing over Mother, a judgmental frown in evidence on my sister's face. "If I no longer respect you, Mother, you have only yourself to blame. Val has nothing to do with it."

Mother's face reddened like a blood sun, and she let out a gasp as if she'd been punched in the heart.

"Don't say anything more you'll come to regret," Dad warned, raising his hand as if to inhibit Ailene.

As I watched my father giving his stern admonition, I had this weird flash of insight. I understood now that he knew about Mother, about her affair with another man. I realized he loved her so much he could forgive her even that. He would seek to protect her and find excuses for her behavior, no matter what.

"Maybe we need family counseling or something," I said.

"Ridiculous," Mother said, folding her arms over her chest.

"We're a dysfunctional family," Ailene said. "Val's right. We ought to see someone, do something."

Mother jumped up and ran, crying, from the room.

Our family conference drew abruptly to an end. Dad hurriedly left the living room, following after Mother.

"I'm going to call Jimmy," Ailene said. "I want to talk to him." She paused on the way out. "Are you okay?"

Wonders never ceased. She was actually concerned. I gave her a weak grin and a nod, and she gave me one of those devastating smiles in return, patting my shoulder on the way out.

Toni came timidly into the living room after Ailene left. I had the impression she had heard at least part of the shouting. We just sat together for a while without saying anything, each lost in our own thoughts. I tried to think about Dave and how happy I was that I finally mattered to him. I thought it would make a big difference. We would be good for each other. I hugged my arms around my body, told myself that things were going to work out with him. But even that thought couldn't remove the sadness I felt about our family problems.

Toni picked up the torn plastic slipcovers and stared at them. "Somebody angry at these?"

"My Dad. He got tired of lies and dishonesty in our family. Shredding the slipcovers was kind of symbolic. Only he couldn't face the total truth in the end."

I could see Toni didn't know what to say.

"Just as well I guess," I continued. "All my life, I wanted to have Mother say, just once, 'I love you. You matter to me.' I don't suppose she ever will."

Toni put her arms around me. I held on to her, and then I did something really stupid, I started to cry. But Toni didn't seem to mind. She just let me continue to hold on to her. When I finally did pull away, I realized that she was crying too. I knew then that she was the only one who really understood how I felt, just as I understood her.

Finally, Toni spoke in a soft voice. "For a long time after my mother left, I hoped she'd come back. I used to pray for it to happen every night. I know now she's never coming back."

The room grew dark. We didn't speak for a long time. Words weren't necessary. It seemed forever before I finally got up and put on a lamp.

"Where's Kathy?"

"I hope you don't mind, she's asleep on your bed. We were watching TV in your room, and she zonked out. The last couple of days have been especially hard for her. Frankly, I'm really scared what tomorrow will be like."

"I'll be there for you," I reassured her. "So will my Dad."

She nodded her head, accepting my words stoically.

A little later, my parents came downstairs. Dad was carrying a suitcase.

"Val, your mother will be staying with Aunt Sandy for a few days. She needs to get away for a little while. We've decided that when she comes back, we're going for some family counseling. I'll make the arrangements."

My mother's face was sad but composed. It looked as if they'd been doing some serious talking.

"Maybe I *have* been wrong about some things." Mother turned to me. "I only wanted what I thought was best for all of us. You've always been a difficult child. When you wouldn't cooperate, I didn't handle it well. I realize that has to change. I have to change. We've all been miserable lately, haven't we? I've got some thinking to do. I know I've hurt you, and I am sorry. You and I, we seem to bring out the worst in each other, don't we? I do want that to end." She offered a tentative, slightly crooked smile.

I realized my parents were both waiting for some sort of a response from me. I wanted to tell her to go straight to the devil. I wanted to say a lot of awful things that would hurt her as much as she'd hurt me. Once, not so long ago, I would have done exactly that. But I wasn't going to say any of it now. Thinking the ugly words was bad enough. Saying them would only make everything worse. So I mentally folded them away in much the manner I'd once collected outgrown clothes from my closet and packaged them for Goodwill.

"I'll try," I said, managing to sound neutral, neither bitter nor hostile.

I had told everyone how I was going to become a better person. Was it possible? I wanted to be valuable, to be valued. Ailene always had a sense of self-worth and entitlement, like it was her birthright. It certainly hadn't been mine. I needed some self-esteem. Still, being a saint or a martyr wasn't really the way for me. I'd done without public approbation and approval this far, why should I need it now? No, if I were going to be a kinder, more compassionate human being, it had to be because it was right for me, because I could better value myself.

First, I had to be able to love myself. Maybe then other people could love me too. Giving love freely without condition was crucial. Being honest about my feelings with Dave had been an important step forward. I'd even managed to reach an accord with Ailene, but could Mother and I ever get along? Our issues were bitter and longstanding. If we reached an accord, it wasn't going to happen in a day, a week, or even a month.

"Being a mother isn't easy. Perhaps you'll find that out one day." Mother was all poise and composure now, determined to win us over with her charm. If she really wanted things to change, then maybe it wasn't too late for our family, but she would have to make some serious changes. Possibly things could work out. Hadn't I already changed, started to grow up?

Mom turned to Dad. "Are you coming?"

"Wait for me in the car, Jan. I'll be right out."

"All right." She first looked from my father to me then left us.

After the front door closed, Dad turned to me. "No one's perfect," he said. When I didn't respond, he seemed compelled to continue. "We're all flawed creatures. So what? It just proves that we're human and fallible."

"I understand that." My throat was tight.

"Do you really understand? Forgiveness is important and necessary."

I gave a quick nod of acceptance. For a moment, our eyes met. Then he left.

I watched him go with mixed feelings spinning around in my head, doing my best to swat them away like a swarm of yellow jackets. I didn't know if my selfish wish had caused all of these changes in my family to occur. Maybe, maybe not. There wasn't any way for me to know for certain. I vowed to be a better daughter and sister, to be kinder, as well as more understanding and forgiving to each of them in the future. I would make amends.

I finally turned to Toni. "Hungry?" I asked.

"Kathy probably is. I'll help you put something together," she said.

"I'd appreciate that."

So, arm in arm, Toni and I set out to do whatever needed to be done.

About the Author

Multiple award-winning author, Jacqueline Seewald, has taught creative, expository, and technical writing at Rutgers University, as well as high school English. She also worked as both an academic librarian and an educational media specialist. Nineteen of her books of fiction have been published to critical praise including books for adults, teens, and children. Her short stories, poems, essays, reviews and articles have appeared in hundreds of diverse publications and numerous anthologies such as: *The Writer, LA Times, Reader's Digest, Pedestal, Sherlock Holmes Mystery Magazine, Over My Dead Body!, Gumshoe Review, Library Journal, Publishers Weekly,* and *The Christian Science Monitor.* Her writer's blog can be found at: http://jacquelineseewald.blogspot.com